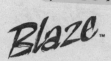

The White Star Continuity
Book 6

DESTINY'S HAND

by

Lori Wilde

The legend concludes… When Morgan and
Adam Shaw jet off to a special vacation to rekindle
their once blazing passion, little do they realize
it'll turn into the adventure of a lifetime. They find
not only *their* second chance, but the chance to
save the charmed amulet known as the White Star!

Dear Reader,

As I was writing *Destiny's Hand,* a story about a couple who've been married ten years and who now find themselves reevaluating the choices they'd made and how those choices have impacted their marriage, I was reminded that my husband and I are quickly approaching our tenth anniversary.

At the decade mark, that first blush of rosy passion has settled into a comfortable enduring love. I might not think about him twenty-four hours a day like before. I no longer stand in the closet sniffing his shirts, filling my nose with his scent as I used to. And some of the things he does, like drinking from the milk carton or interrupting me when I'm writing, get on my nerves. But without fail, whenever he walks into the room not only does my heart beat faster, but my whole world lights up.

I posed myself a set of questions. What if a couple who desperately loved each other had drifted apart, but had no idea how to find their way back to each other? How do they again get the magic that makes their hearts beat fast and their whole lives light up? Once the magic is gone, is it lost forever? Or is it possible, through love and communication, to create a whole new level of magic, far brighter and greater than anything the lovers have ever known before?

These questions were both exciting and challenging to explore. Adam and Morgan Shaw took me on their roller-coaster ride with them. And when the book was over, you know what I did? To my husband's great delight, I set about rekindling a little of that magic for ourselves.

Be romantic, dear readers. Fill every day with love!

Lori Wilde

DESTINY'S HAND

Lori Wilde

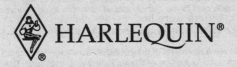

HARLEQUIN®

TORONTO • NEW YORK • LONDON
AMSTERDAM • PARIS • SYDNEY • HAMBURG
STOCKHOLM • ATHENS • TOKYO • MILAN • MADRID
PRAGUE • WARSAW • BUDAPEST • AUCKLAND

If you purchased this book without a cover you should be aware that this book is stolen property. It was reported as "unsold and destroyed" to the publisher, and neither the author nor the publisher has received any payment for this "stripped book."

To Betty Werner, a fabulous artist.
Thank you for your talent and the gifts from your heart.

ISBN 0-373-79264-6

DESTINY'S HAND

Copyright © 2006 by Laurie Vanzura.

All rights reserved. Except for use in any review, the reproduction or utilization of this work in whole or in part in any form by any electronic, mechanical or other means, now known or hereafter invented, including xerography, photocopying and recording, or in any information storage or retrieval system, is forbidden without the written permission of the publisher, Harlequin Enterprises Limited, 225 Duncan Mill Road, Don Mills, Ontario, Canada M3B 3K9.

All characters in this book have no existence outside the imagination of the author and have no relation whatsoever to anyone bearing the same name or names. They are not even distantly inspired by any individual known or unknown to the author, and all incidents are pure invention.

This edition published by arrangement with Harlequin Books S.A.

® and TM are trademarks of the publisher. Trademarks indicated with ® are registered in the United States Patent and Trademark Office, the Canadian Trade Marks Office and in other countries.

www.eHarlequin.com

Printed in U.S.A.

THE LEGEND CONCLUDES

Egmath knew he was dying.

His vision was gone, his limbs numb and useless, his blood seeping away from him, soaking into the hot desert sand. But the wicked sword that had mortally pierced his heart in the heat of fierce battle had not destroyed his soul.

One thought. One single precious thought dominated his essence.

Batu.

His beloved.

He thought of her sweet voice, her delicate scent, the feel of her soft lips upon his. How silky was her hair. How creamy her skin. But those were not the reasons he loved her. He loved her sharp mind and her tender laugh and the way she made him feel special. He loved her courage and her determination. He loved the way she had respected his code of honor and had not asked him to violate it. Not even so they could be together.

Batu.

He thought of the way they'd played in the cypress grove as children, laughing and teasing each other. He recalled how their love had grown as they'd grown older. The first kiss they'd shared. The love they'd made. He remembered the pain of learning that he must marry her sister, that in this life Batu could never be his. For that reason alone he was glad this incarnation was over.

Egmath had known her and loved her from a time beyond time. She was his soul mate. They were fused. One. It did not matter that duty demanded he marry her sister, Anan. Batu was forever his and he was hers. They were two halves of a whole. Nothing could tear them asunder.

Not even death.

He felt no pain, for his love for Batu sustained him as he left the world, his spirit flying far above the battlefield. Taking him to a place of quiet peace, a place where he knew the truth.

Only love was real.

The one eternal constant.

Finally he let go, completely severing the thin silver thread anchoring his soul to his body. Knowing everything was all right. Knowing that one day, he and his beloved would be together again.

For she was his destiny.

Arik, Egmath's second in command, was wounded, but not mortally so. Bleeding and in pain, he staggered through the horror of the battlefield. He examined the bodies, searching for his leader and praying to the gods that Egmath, the greatest warrior who'd ever lived, had somehow managed to survive the carnage.

"Egmath," he shouted over and over, but the only sounds that met his call were the sounds of men dying.

After a long search, his heart tightened in his chest when he caught sight of Egmath's familiar tunic fluttering in the wind. He dropped onto his knees in the sand beside Egmath's body, grief twisting tears from his eyes. Egmath stared sightlessly at the sky, but he had a beatific smile on his face, as if he'd seen something glorious calling to him from the other side.

Egmath had been not only Arik's leader, but his best friend, confiding things to him that he confided to no one else. Arik knew about Batu. He knew about the White Star amulet.

The amulet. Where was the amulet? Egmath would want him to take it back to Batu. But the amulet was no longer around his neck where he normally wore it. Arik checked Egmath's tunic to see if the White Star had been torn from the leather strap and fallen into his clothing but he could not find it. Feeling almost frantic, as if he were letting down his friend in the one time he needed him most, Arik rolled Egmath's body over and searched the ground beneath him.

No amulet.

He gently rolled him back over. "I'm sorry, my old friend. I let you down."

And then something caught his eye.

Egmath was clutching something tightly in his hands.

Arik slowly pried Egmath's fingers open. What he saw there was not the White Star amulet.

But something far more valuable to Egmath's beloved Batu.

Arik knew what he must do. He would take this to Batu and protect it with his life.

1

"ARE YOU ABSOLUTELY certain this is the way to get the magic back?" Morgan Shaw whispered urgently into her slim black flip phone.

On the sidewalk outside the Grand Duchess, a fashionable boutique hotel located on Manhattan's Upper East Side, Morgan paced in the gentle breeze of an early September evening. In her estimation, she was dressed, to put it quite succinctly, like a hooker. Tight black leather miniskirt, stretchy red Lycra top with a plunging neckline and Julia Roberts' *Pretty Woman* thigh-high boots. She wore too much makeup, not nearly enough lingerie and an auburn wig that made her scalp itch.

And every time she stalked past the discreet front entrance of the Grand Duchess, the top-hat-wearing doorman shot her a one-wrong-move-doxy-and-I'll-sic-the-cops-on-you glower.

Morgan tugged at the hem of her miniskirt in a desperate attempt to make it look longer, to make herself feel less mortified.

"Stoking sexual desire is the first step in recapturing

the magic," lectured her younger sister, Cass, who was on the other end of the cell phone conversation. "Ultimately it's all about the hot sex."

"There's hot sex and then there's—" Morgan peered down at her skimpy attire and shook her head "—just plain hot to trot."

"Hey, hey." Cass read her thoughts. "Those were my best going-out clothes before I met Sam."

"Exactly. That's what terrifies me."

"Need I remind you, sister dearest, that you were the one who came to me for advice?"

"No, you're right. I can do this," Morgan said, feeling as jittery as if someone had forcibly injected her with pure Colombian coffee-bean extract.

"Sure you can. Be bold, be brave, be bewitching."

"That's easy for you to say. You're already all those things."

"You can be, too."

"I don't know about that," Morgan mumbled. She stepped back against the wall of a nearby residential building to get out of the way of foot traffic. "Decking out like a Victoria's Secret model seems so overstated."

"You've tried understated and it really hasn't had the desired effect you were going for now, has it? Do you want the magic back or not?"

"Of course I do."

"Then for crying out loud, if you want to snag Adam's attention, you're going to have to do something big and dramatic."

The concept sounded so sensible when Cass vocalized it, but to Morgan it seemed the emotional equivalent of using a flamethrower to light a votive candle. Serious overkill.

"But exactly how do I go about doing that?"

"Fantasy."

"Excuse me?"

"Come on, work with me here. Imagine that Adam is a lonesome cowpoke who aches to learn how to read and you're the new schoolmarm who's going to tutor him all night long. And I do mean all night long."

"Ugh."

"Okay, so that's one of my fantasies. Pick your own. Pirate and captive. Biker dude and uptight socialite. Stable boy and countess. Whatever gets your juices flowing."

What did get her juices flowing? It was an important question to which Morgan had no immediate answer. She hadn't really thought about it all that much. As a practical woman, she wasn't big on unrealistic fantasies and she said as much to her sister.

"That's why they're called fantasies, precisely because they are unrealistic. Jeez, Morg, don't you ever just let yourself have a little fun?"

"But if I have to go to such crazy lengths to snag my husband's attention, doesn't it mean that he's no longer attracted to me? What if it's just the wig and the clothes that jump-start his spark plugs? Or worse yet, what if he resents me trying to seduce him?" That idea had

Morgan pulling her bottom lip, painted Serious Scarlet, between her teeth in consternation.

"You're overthinking this. Men are simple creatures. Give 'em hot sex and cold beer and competitive sports and they're happy. Now go blow your man's mind," Cass said and hung up.

It was a sad state of affairs when you had to ask your unmarried baby sister for advice on how to revive your sex life.

Morgan's palms were so slick with nervous sweat she fumbled her cell phone, almost dropping it before finally getting the clasp open and slipping it into her vintage beaded handbag. She ran her palms over her hips to dry them.

A little over a year ago she'd been just like Adam, working eighty hours a week, reaching for the brass ring, striving to make their financial goals a reality so they could buy their dream home and start a family. They'd been a team then, both so enmeshed in their climb to the top of the corporate ladder that there had been little time to consider the personal sacrifices they'd been making in order to achieve their objectives.

And then two things had happened.

First, she'd driven by a charming antique store in Fairfield, Connecticut, where she and Adam were looking to buy their first home and spied a For Sale sign in the window. Excitement, fresh and unexpected, had pushed through her as a little voice in the back of her head whispered, *buy it.*

She ignored the voice, tamped down the excitement. Owning an antique store was not part of the plan. But still, she couldn't forget the unbridled joy she'd felt at the thought of it. She always had an affinity for both history and objets d'art and her mind spun cozy fantasies of finding just the right pieces for her customers who she would get to know on a first-name basis. She would make the shop homey and inviting, serve complimentary coffee and hot tea. She liked the idea of being part of a smaller community, of being connected to the past in such a tangible way.

The second thing that caused Morgan to revaluate her life in a significant way was a major accounting scandal that rocked the financial world. Her firm, where she managed multimillion-dollar mutual funds, ended up being probed during a federal investigation. Her company had been signing off on accounts without really doing the mandatory auditing work, allowing creative cheating to slip past unnoticed. Morgan was not involved, but some of her colleagues had been. Their excuse was that they'd been stretched too thin to adequately monitor every account. Her firm was levied a huge fine and several people lost their jobs. While her company hadn't done anything outright criminal, they'd been negligent in their practices.

The scandal affected her far more deeply than she realized. She had trouble sleeping and she spent hours questioning her morals, values and long held beliefs. How could she, in good conscience, continue to work for a corporation that didn't serve their clients with the due diligence they deserved?

She discussed her concerns with Adam and then she'd sprung the idea of buying the antique shop. She was heartened when he said he was behind her one hundred percent. His support gave her the courage to turn in her resignation, buy the antique shop and pursue her dream.

Leaving the job she'd held for nine years had not been easy. She felt scared and uncertain, especially in the beginning when she had a lot of money going out and none coming in, but ultimately the trade-off had been more than worth it. She'd grown in ways she couldn't have imagined and she'd come to treasure the extra time her new job afforded her.

But while the shop was now turning a profit and their new home in Connecticut was everything she'd ever hoped for, her relationship with Adam was faltering. They were no longer a team. Adam was still climbing. Reaching, ever reaching for that elusive dream of "enough" that Morgan had already discovered by giving up the chase.

She had wanted so badly to share her newfound sense of freedom and inner peace with her beloved husband, but no matter how hard she tried to tell him what she was thinking and feeling, he just couldn't seem to get it. She felt sorry for herself that she'd lost her teammate, but even sorrier for Adam because he was still running a race that could not be won.

They were drifting further and further apart and she longed for the carefree teasing of their early days. She missed the easy camaraderie of a lazy Sunday morning spent leisurely strolling hand-in-hand through Central Park. Or piling up on the couch together, legs entwined as they worked the New York Times crossword puzzle and fed each other tidbits of sweet pastries or sectioned fruit.

Morgan sighed. She was determined to bridge the chasm before it was too late.

To that end, she had scheduled a romantic two-week vacation in the Loire Valley in France for their tenth wedding anniversary, planning on returning to the country where they had honeymooned. Secretly she'd been learning French as a surprise for Adam. He'd always admired her thirst for knowledge and self-improvement.

But when Adam had called her that afternoon to say he would be staying in Manhattan because he had an eight o'clock business meeting at the Grand Duchess, Morgan realized she couldn't wait for the trip to revive their flagging love life. It was the second time this week and the twelfth time in the last month that Adam had chosen to stay in the city overnight.

No more wishing and hoping things would improve on their own or that Adam would have his own epiphany the way she'd had. She had to take action.

Now.

Which was why she was here, dressed like a trollop, treading a groove in Eighty-first Street and woefully second-guessing herself.

She checked her watch.

It was seven forty-five. Not much time. But she didn't need much time. She just wanted Adam to see what was going to be waiting for him upstairs in his hotel room when his business meeting finished.

"Hey, babe." A good-looking man in an expensive business suit stopped on the sidewalk beside her. "You interested in a little somethin', somethin'?"

Morgan blasted him with the coldest stare she could marshal, making a scalding laser of her eyes, and the guy slunk off like a cowed dog, palms raised and mumbling an apology.

Head held high, she swept haughtily past the portly doorman—who was still eyeing her suspiciously—and stepped through the revolving door into the lobby of the Grand Duchess. But then she went and ruined her staged bravado by stumbling in Cass's stiletto boots.

Aha, exposed for the fraud she was. No femme fatale, Morgan Shaw.

Determined not to let her vulnerability show, she tossed her fake auburn hair and stalked toward the lounge.

Her heels clacked too loudly against the marble floor. The significance of this step weighed importantly upon her heart.

What if her ploy failed?

Prudence whispered inside her head, *Morgan, let sleeping dogs lie. Go back home before he sees you. Things aren't that bad. Adam is a good man. He loves you. You love him. Forget this awful need for something more, something magical. It's a myth, a fairy tale. Grow up, for God's sake, and face reality.*

How much easier it would be if she could flee, but she possessed the strangest notion that if she turned back now, something inside her would die forever.

Morgan entered the bar and stood in the doorway, letting her eyes adjust to the darker lighting, her gaze wandering around the room in search of her husband. She spotted him seated in a corner booth, head down, brow furrowed, paperwork spread out on the table in front of him.

Her heart hiccuped, reeling drunkenly on fear and possibilities.

He was so handsome with his sturdy all-American good looks. Thick sandy-blond hair cut short but not severely so. Clean shaven. Affable cheekbones, intelligent blue eyes, strong chin, absolutely perfect nose.

He'd played football in high school. Quarterback, naturally. And Adam had managed to hang on to his lean waist and muscular chest. It came at a price, however. Daily morning jogs, weekends on the weight machines at the gym, no sleeping in late and spooning with her. But he considered the results worth the sacrifice.

Morgan hoped their future children would look exactly like him—that is, if they ever managed to have kids with the way things were going. She'd never thought she was pretty enough for Adam. On the looks meter, her handsome husband was a solid nine, while she considered herself a six at best.

She was on the bony side, small boobs, narrow hips, definitely not the sort of woman that men could sink their hands into. Her own hair was fine and blond and wouldn't hold a style. She considered her bright brown eyes her best feature. And while friends had told her she resembled the actress Joan Allen, Morgan couldn't help thinking they were extremely generous with their compliments.

Adam glanced toward the door, no doubt scouting for his client, and quickly flicked his gaze over her, not even recognizing his own wife.

Her pulse spiked and doubt sank its vicious teeth into her. This was bad timing. She'd made a mistake in coming here.

She almost ran away.

But the thought of catching the train back to that big empty house in Connecticut stopped her. She was tired of feeling lonely, tired of feeling disconnected, of feeling as if she'd somehow left her husband behind. She wanted him on her team again, wanted their hearts and minds to meld on a higher plane. She wanted the full extent of the happily-ever-after promise and she wanted it today.

Emboldened by the notion that she could have what she longed for, Morgan stalked across the lounge toward him, purposefully putting a seductive sway into her step.

Her heart beat harder and faster the closer she came to the high-backed conch-shell-shaped private booth where Adam sat.

Steady, steady. Don't invest the outcome with more significance than it deserves. It's just one step.

Yes, but in what direction?

Toward reunion?

Or divorce?

Morgan exhaled, unable to believe she had allowed the D word to pop into her head for even a fraction of a second.

Adam had already returned his attention to his paperwork. The booth lamp cast a shadow over his profile. His eyes drank in the words on the page. In his right hand he clutched the expensive ballpoint pen she had bought him as a Christmas present two years ago. His tailored silk suit hugged his shoulders, and he had loosened the tie at his neck.

She slipped into the cushioned seat across from him.

"Buy a girl a drink?" she said in the huskiest voice she could manage and leaned forward to accent her cleavage induced by her new padded push-up bra.

"Huh?" Adam blinked owlishly and stared at her as if she were a stranger.

Her chest tightened at the startled expression in his eyes. A heated flush of awkwardness climbed up her throat and burned her cheeks.

"Morgan?"

"Surprise." She smiled shakily, scared as a kid on her first roller coaster ride.

She studied him intently, looking for some sign of arousal, of sexual interest, of basic male attraction. But Adam revealed neither delight nor approval. She could see nothing beyond his investment banker's poker face. Nothing that said he saw her as a sexy, desirable woman.

Come on, what did you expect? For him to throw you down on the table and have his way with you right here in the bar? You of all people should understand what kind of mental stress he's under. You've been there. Cut him some slack.

Yes, she knew what he was going through and that was precisely the reason she was here. To shake things up, to get him to see all the wonderful experiences he was missing out on by focusing so much of his time and energy on work to the exclusion of everything else.

"Um…what are you doing here?" His brow bunched in a frown, and he rubbed the back of his neck with a palm in a gesture she recognized. He was trying to ease the knots of tension wadding up under his skin. "And what is that you're wearing?"

Adam's jaw tightened, as if he wanted to say more but was gnawing on the words to keep them from tumbling out. His gaze skated over Morgan's scandalous attire, but then he averted his eyes as if her being here made him uncomfortable.

The clothes were too much. Over the top. She knew that now. Had known it from the beginning, actually, but she'd let herself be persuaded by Cass. Image mattered a lot to Adam, and she had just embarrassed him at a place where he was well known, where he conducted business.

"I thought…I thought…"

Every silly thought she'd had about surprising him, making him crazy with desire and having wild sex at the Grand Duchess flew right out of her head. Good God, what had she been thinking? Interrupting his work with her lame attempt at seduction? The whole thing seemed cheesy now, ridiculous. This was what happened when she listened to her sister.

She'd been so stupid. This wasn't the right way to get him to see her point of view.

Ducking her head in shame, she let her hair fall across her face, hoping it would hide the concern in her eyes. She slapped both palms against the smooth, cool marble tabletop and levered her butt up off the padded leather seat.

"I'm just going to go now. I'm sorry I interrupted you."

"Morgan." Adam reached out to touch her. But just before his hand settled over hers, a bulky man with a pit-bull face sidled up to their table.

"Is this a bad time, Shaw?"

"Robert." Adam got to his feet and shook his client's hand. "You're here."

"Eight o'clock right on the money, punctual as always. But you look as if you've been caught unaware." Robert stared at Morgan with frank approval.

Dammit. That's the way she wanted her husband to look at her, not this overweight, middle-aged stranger.

Adam cleared his throat, rubbed the flat of one hand against the back of his neck again. "Um, Robert, this is my wife, Morgan. Morgan, this is Robert Jacobbi of Jacobbi Enterprises."

Pasting a civilized smile on her lips, Morgan shook the man's hand.

"So this is your wife." Jacobbi wriggled his eyebrows. They were so thick and bushy they looked like gray caterpillars dancing the conga. "Shaw, if you don't mind my saying, you're one lucky guy."

"If you could give us just a second, Robert, I'll be right with you. Have a seat. Order a drink."

"You're not joining us, Morgan?" Jacobbi's eyes glistened as he settled himself into the seat she had just vacated.

"I was on my way home."

"Well, it was my absolute pleasure to have met you, Mrs. Shaw," he said.

Adam took her hand and guided her out of Jacobbi's earshot. His eyes held hers, his body stiffened, his whisper was rough. "What's going on? Where did you get those clothes?"

"Cass."

"Ah, so that explains it."

"This isn't Cass's fault," she snapped. "I had a silly idea that it would be romantic to spend the night with you in the city, and my sister loaned me something sexy to wear."

His hand stole along her bare arm tenderly and his tone softened. "And you look exceptional, but you know how it is. You've been through this before. If I ace this deal with Jacobbi I'm a shoo-in for my promotion. But if I blow it, I'll be passed over."

"I realize that. It's just…" She stopped, at a loss as to how to tell him how much she missed him, how afraid she was that the magic had gone out of their marriage and how terrified she was that they were on the verge of losing each other.

But this wasn't the time or the place. She had embarrassed them both enough for one day.

"Just what?" he asked, sounding impatient.

"We'll talk later. Go back to your client." She waved a wrist, trying not to let him see her eyes, trying not to reveal her fragility.

"Are you sure you're all right?" There was real concern in his voice. "This is totally out of character for you."

I know! she wanted to scream.

Didn't he get it? That was the point. To step out of character. To be someone else, someone new, someone wild and adventuresome and sexy.

Adam took off his suit jacket and held it out to her. "Here, you can't go walking around the city at night alone dressed like that."

She slipped her arms through the jacket. He hadn't criticized her, but the expression on his face seemed to say it all: *I hope this behavior isn't going to become a habit. I chose you as my wife because you're calm and reliable and sensible. Don't go pulling any purple rabbits out of a hat on me at this late date.*

"Jacobbi's waiting," she said, her chest squeezing sorrowfully.

"You be careful going home." He gave her a perfunctory kiss.

The brushing of his lips against her skin felt so damned brotherly she could barely stand it. Quickly she turned away, glad that she wasn't the kind of woman who cried at the drop of a hat.

Her humiliation was quite complete enough without tears.

WHAT THE HELL HAD THAT been about?

Stunned by his restrained wife's unexpected conduct, Adam slipped into the booth across from Robert Jacobbi. He was rattled, thrown off his game and fretful at the thought of Morgan taking the train home dressed in those high-heeled boots and skimpy clothes.

At least she had on his coat. He used the rationalization to placate his concern, but his gut torqued.

His gaze lingered on the exit where Morgan had just disappeared. He wished he'd handled things differently, wished he hadn't been so worried that everyone in the bar was thinking that he had ordered himself up a high-class escort.

"I'll have a scotch, no ice," Jacobbi told the cocktail waitress who wandered over.

"Make that two," Adam said.

He would have preferred mineral water. He didn't drink much. He felt that alcohol clouded his concentration. And when he did imbibe, he preferred beer to hard liquor. But liquor was an elementary ingredient in the art of sealing a deal. Adam had learned to drink whatever his client was having whether he liked it or not.

"Your wife seems very nice," Jacobbi said. "I liked her."

"She is wonderful and she's unlike any woman I've ever known. Understanding, patient."

"And very sexy."

"Yeah," Adam smiled. "That, too."

He thought of Morgan and his heart immediately warmed. Her features possessed plenty of character, with brown eyes too big for her face that underscored her natural curiosity about the world. Her bottom lip was full, but her top lip was so narrow it almost disappeared whenever she smiled, and he adored that sweet disappearing act.

But it was her chin that Adam loved most.

Small and rounded but prominent, and when Morgan hardened it, you could be sure you were in for a protracted argument. *I might be all dainty and ladylike on the outside, but inside, I'm pure steel,* her stubborn chin seemed to say.

Adam remembered the first time he laid eyes on her. He'd walked into his senior-level economics class in business school and there she'd been. Sitting in the first row, where he preferred to sit. The other students were talking and joking, waiting for class to begin. But Morgan sat perfectly still.

She was an island, untouched by the chaotic sea around her. Quiet, serene.

Her calm reserve had captured him immediately. Adam was not a particularly deep or spiritual person. He realized this about himself, and his rather surface approach to life didn't bother him. In fact, the trait was an asset in his line of work. But something about Morgan caused a voice inside his head to whisper, *Here it is, the thing you never even knew was missing.*

He admired her neat and tidy methods. The way she preferred everything clean and organized. On the surface, she was very controlled, his Morgan, but underneath her composure, at times like tonight, he would catch a glimpse of her inner vixen.

"To be frank," Jacobbi commented, "if she were my wife, willing to dress up like that for me, I'd be spending every night of the week with her. But then, I shouldn't be talking about your wife that way. Excuse me. It's none of my business what shape your marriage is in."

"My marriage isn't in bad shape," Adam denied.

"No?"

Vehemently he shook his head. "No."

"So why are you here with me instead of at home with her?"

"Because you asked for a late meeting."

"Ever consider telling me to shove it and meet at a time that didn't disrupt your family life?"

"Would you be my client if I did?"

"Maybe not. The point is that you have to make choices in this world, Shaw. And it's clear you've chosen business over family. Nothing wrong with that. Just make no mistake—you'll pay top dollar for your sacrifices."

"Speaking from experience, Jacobbi?"

"I'm on wife number three, my kids won't speak to me, but I'm a millionaire several times over. You figure it out."

"Two scotches for the gentlemen," the waitress said and settled their drinks in front of them.

Adam signed the drinks to his hotel room. Pensively he sipped from his glass. Was Jacobbi right? Was he paying too high of a price for success?

But I'm doing it for Morgan, so she can have her antique shop. For our home. For the kids we don't yet have.

He looked across the table at the older man and suddenly flashed fifteen years in the future. Would he still be doing this job at Jacobbi's age—accommodating big-fish clients by meeting them late at night, even when it wasn't conducive to his home life, simply to make more money?

The thought unsettled him.

So do something about it.

Now?

Adam glanced around as if someone was watching him, gauging his response, critiquing his choices.

His heart urged him to make his excuses to Jacobbi, reschedule their meeting and go home to his wife. But he was so very close to being made vice president. If he pissed off Jacobbi, he could jeopardize the promotion he had been working his entire life to snag. If he was going to distinguish himself above the other VP candidates, he had to go above and beyond the call of duty, not wimp out at the last moment.

Not even for the sake of your marriage?

Come on. His marriage was fine. No matter what Jacobbi had said. Sure, maybe their sex life had slowed down over the years, but hell, he and Morgan had been married a decade. It was normal and natural for the excitement to wax and wane.

Yet no matter how much Adam tried to convince himself that things were perfectly fine at home, he couldn't stop remembering the look in Morgan's eyes when he'd asked her what she was doing there. He'd hurt her feelings, and that had not been his intention.

Should he stay or should he go?

"Let's get down to business," Jacobbi said, rubbing his palms together and launching into details about his plans for taking his company public.

The next thing Adam knew, he was caught up in the minutiae, talking shop. But in the back of his head he made a decision. He wouldn't stay at the Grand Duchess tonight as he'd planned. Even if the meeting ran so late that he missed the last train out of the city, he would spring for taxi fare to Connecticut. One way or the other, he was going to make love to his wife tonight.

He was determined to prove to them both that their marriage was one hundred percent okay.

2

Morgan arrived home to find the green light on the answering machine blinking provocatively. Could it be Adam calling to say that he'd changed his mind and was coming home tonight after all? Her heart cartwheeled with hope.

Please let it be him, she prayed.

Unzipping Cass's slut-puppy boots, Morgan kicked them across the entryway floor. She stripped off the itchy red wig, tossed it onto the foyer table and ran her fingers through her damp hair. She still wore Adam's jacket, the sleeves dangling past her fingertips.

While pulling up one sleeve, she reached over to press the play button on the machine. Blood drained from her legs and pooled throbbing into her toes. Whether from anticipation of the message on the machine or from spending several hours in those unaccustomed high-heeled boots, she did not know for sure, but probably it was a bit of both.

"Hello, Morgan, this is Sam Mason returning your call."

Her hopes took a sucker punch.

Detective Sergeant Sam Mason was Cass's new boyfriend. Down-to-earth Sam was good for her flighty baby sister, and for that fact alone Morgan adored him. It was the first serious relationship Cass had ever had, and whenever Morgan saw the two of them together, she couldn't help longing for the kind of fire-blazing passion they shared.

"In answer to your inquiry, no, I'm afraid the White Star amulet is no longer in the possession of the NYPD," Sam's voice spun out into the room.

Morgan had telephoned Sam that afternoon, before heading over to the Grand Duchess, in response to information she had received the previous morning from an archaeologist named Cate Wells. Several months ago Morgan had found an intriguing antique box in the basement of her antique shop, along with an ancient French text about an amulet that had belonged to star-crossed lovers.

At first, Morgan had found the box merely intriguing, but as time passed and she unearthed bits and pieces of the legend, she had become obsessed with finding out the truth about the box, the book and the White Star amulet, which had been stolen last April from the Stanhope auction house.

Sam had been assigned to the case and that was how he'd gotten involved with her sister. Cass had taken the book to him when she and Morgan had realized the stolen amulet was the same one pictured in the book.

Morgan had found the tome among the antiques she'd purchased in a lot along with her shop.

Pieces of the puzzle had slowly started to come together, revealing a fascinating legend of star-crossed lovers and the magical power of true love.

Cate Wells had taken photos of the box and then shown them to an expert in the field. He had confirmed the connection, speculating that indeed the star-shaped design on the box correlated with a star-shaped key.

It was in that moment it occurred to Morgan that the White Star amulet was probably the key that opened the box. The key, that last Morgan had heard, was locked up in the evidence room at the Thirty-ninth Precinct, where Sam worked.

"No one knows where the amulet is," Sam's taped message continued. "There's an investigation under way, but it's looking like a dirty cop took a bribe to steal it for someone else. That's all I can tell you right now. The station is in an uproar."

Darn it. Morgan sighed and swallowed her second big disappointment of the day. Another dead end.

Still, she wasn't a quitter. Once she sank her teeth into something, she hung on until there was absolutely no possibility of victory.

She belonged to an online message board for antique dealers, and there was a thread about stolen antiquities. What would it hurt to make a few discreet inquiries? She'd already posted about the box once before when she was trying to learn precisely what it might be and who its previous owners could have been.

All she would have to do was leave a message saying she'd discovered that a very unique key opened the box. She would try dangling the box as bait for the person who now possessed the amulet.

It was a long shot and she knew it, but Morgan was glad to have something to focus on besides her failed seduction.

She stripped off her sexy clothes—which seemed particularly pathetic in light of what had *not* happened at the Grand Duchess—scrubbed the heavy makeup off her face and slipped into her favorite pair of silk pajamas. Feeling more like herself again, she poured herself a glass of wine, padded into her home office and booted up her computer.

Logging on to the message board took a few minutes. Then she spent a long while getting the wording of her e-mail just right before she was satisfied enough to post it to the group.

She signed the missive *Curious in Connecticut* and entered "Special Gem" in the subject line. Satisfied, she depressed the send button, leaned back in her plush leather chair and took a long sip of Pinot Grigio. The slightly sweet liquid flowed warmly through her body, easing her tension.

A few minutes later her post popped up on the message board.

"It'll probably be months before I get a response," she muttered gloomily.

She searched through other threads, looking for posts of interest, but found nothing related to ancient amulets or long-lost boxes. Melancholy weighted her shoulders. She wrapped her sadness around her like a cloak, drank it in with the wine until her body pulsed, encompassed by the feeling.

Here it was again, the blue funk that whispered darkly to her in moments of doubt and shame. These feelings did not express who she thought she should be. What was wrong with her? She adored her husband. Why this desperate wish for something deeper?

Why? Because while she had transformed herself from an overworked, overachiever into a woman who was finally satisfied with her own life, it tortured her not to be able to share her personal growth with Adam. She wanted him to join her on this exciting path of liberation. She wanted him to understand how much more fulfilled he could be if he would just slow down and reconnect with the world around him. She longed for a more spiritual bond between them.

Picking up the box that she kept displayed on her desk, she studied it carefully as she had every day since she'd found it.

Intricate hand-carved symbols and designs that looked as if they could be some kind of hieroglyphics whiskered the box made from bubinga wood and darkened with age. The faint fragrance of some rich, exotic spice emanated from it. Morgan traced her fingers across the lid, over elaborate grooves where the expert archaeologist had said was the likely place to open the box with a star-shaped key.

Now that she had learned fresh details about the legend, she was even more fascinated than before. Between translating the old French tome with her new language skills and talking to experts in several disciplines, she had slowly pieced together the legend of the star-crossed lovers.

Three thousand years ago, in a now-vanished desert kingdom, Egmath and Batu had secretly been meeting every evening under the midnight stars near a grove of cypress trees. They shared their dreams, ambitions, lives and eventually their real feelings for one another. Theirs was a pure love, a true love. But alas, it could never be. In accordance with ancient custom, the kingdom's bravest warrior, Egmath, was chosen to marry Batu's older sister, Princess Anan, who had become queen.

Egmath spent the evening before his wedding to Anan with his beloved Batu, when she presented him with an amulet she had secretly commissioned. It was made of ivory and fashioned in the shape of a five-pointed star with a hollowed-out center.

With the amulet tightly pressed between their entwined hands, Egmath and Batu vowed their everlasting love to each other. That night, beneath the magic of the moon and the optimism of the stars, Egmath and Batu made love for the first and only time. The amulet blazed brightly. According to the fable, it now held the power of true love for whoever possessed it and was pure of heart.

The story was so sad. Soul mates destined to be together but torn asunder by their culture's tradition and Egmath's sense of honor.

Wasn't that just like a man? Placing duty over love. Morgan snorted.

And poor Anan? What about her? Hadn't the woman deserved a man who loved her the way that Egmath had loved Batu?

If Morgan closed her eyes, she could see Anan in her marriage, believing it was solid, knowing that she had a good man in Egmath. But somewhere in the back of her mind, as Anan went about her royal duties, she was bound to have nagging doubts. She was certain to realize the connection between herself and her new husband was not as it should be.

Did Anan wonder what he was thinking when she caught Egmath staring longingly out across the desert? Did she question his love for her when he wouldn't tell her where he'd gotten the amulet that he wore around his neck and never took off? Did she doubt herself as a woman when he would kiss her perfunctorily, sweetly but without any real hint of passion?

Morgan sighed and opened her eyes.

Maybe she was obsessed with the box and the legend because it represented the magic that was sorely missing from her own marriage. It wasn't the first time she'd had such thoughts.

And what if she located the amulet and opened the

box only to find nothing there? That it was as empty inside as she was?

What then?

The thought startled her.

What on earth was she doing? Posting that message had been a bad idea. She should forget about the legend and just concentrate on building a stronger marriage. She had to stop using the mystery of the box as a buffer for her feelings, as a barrier to keep from facing what was going on in her own life.

Quick, delete the post before it's too late.

Morgan leaned forward and was about to zap the message into cyberspace when another post popped up in the Special Gem thread.

"Twinkle, Twinkle Little Star" read the enigmatic subject line.

Morgan's breath caught and her stomach staggered. Desire rose in her, the famished need to have her curiosity sated. Whether she wanted to admit her compulsion or not, she had to find out what was in that box.

Her hand hovered over the mouse. She'd never expected a response so swiftly.

Or one so cagey.

It appeared that someone knew the special gem she had written about was the White Star. Could the electronic posting possibly be from the person who currently possessed the amulet?

She was surprised to find her fingers trembling as she clicked the cursor on the read tab.

Dear Curious in Connecticut,
I might have access to what you're looking for. If I may ask, what is the nature of your interest in the piece? Please answer through private e-mail.

It was unsigned.

Morgan's heart stilled and a strange sense of calm came over her, even as the rational voice in the back of her head warned her not to get too excited or jump to erroneous conclusions.

After months of searching, was she within days of opening the box?

Her fingers flew over the keyboard as she poured out her findings into the e-mail. She launched into detail, describing how she believed the amulet might be the key that opened the box. Her breath came in raspy backward gasps as she signed her real name and hit Send.

Morgan got up and walked back and forth in front of the computer screen, thrill pumping a shower of tingles throughout her body. "Come on, come on, please answer me back."

Five minutes passed, then ten. She paced the room, one hand splayed against the hollow of her throat. It wasn't until she began to feel light-headed that Morgan realized she wasn't exhaling.

Breathe.

She took a deep, cleansing yoga breath. Why did it feel as if the key to her future lay in this stranger's response?

Finally after several long, agonizing minutes, the

cheery digitized voice on her computer announced, "You've got mail."

Morgan flung herself back into the chair and opened the letter.

All wariness had vanished from the sender's earlier post.

Dear Morgan,
It sounds as if you have the same obsession with unique antiques as I. If you are willing to make your intriguing box available to me, then I'll provide the amulet and we could open the box together. When would it be possible for us to meet? I live on the Mediterranean Sea in a small fishing village not far from Nice, but I am not in the best of health and unable to travel abroad. If you would consider a trip to France, you are welcome to stay at my villa. I would much enjoy a long chat with a kindred spirit.
Sincerely yours,
Henri Renouf

The hairs on Morgan's forearm lifted and a chill chased up her spine. Could this guy be on the up-and-up? Did he really have access to the White Star? Or was he some weirdo who surfed the Net looking to lure unsuspecting women to France?

Morgan composed another post, telling him that she hoped he wouldn't be offended by her inquiry, but a woman couldn't be too cautious and she would require some reassurance that he was a legitimate dealer and that he had actually seen the White Star. She asked him to describe the amulet.

Minutes later his reply came back.

I appreciate your hesitation. It is only prudent in this electronic age to question the identity and motive of the person behind the post. I have been dealing in antiquities for many years and across many continents. My specialties are antique firearms, rare talismans with intriguing histories and unique North African objets d'art, which is how the White Star came into my possession. The amulet is very lovely. It is a five-pointed star made of the purest snow-white ivory and it is about the size of a petite woman's palm, with a hollow center. However, anyone could know this if he or she had done the research, so let me suggest that you check my credentials. Perhaps that would convince you that I am genuine.

Morgan inhaled sharply. His description accurately matched the illustration of the White Star that she and Cass had stumbled across in the old French tome and then read about in an article in the *New York Times* when it had been stolen from the Stanhope auction house. The amulet had been recovered, but then it had been stolen from a museum, found again and was now currently missing from the evidence room at Sam's precinct. She couldn't help but wonder if Henri Renouf knew something about the thefts that he wasn't telling.

Had he obtained the White Star through illegal means? It seemed likely. Yet everyone was innocent until proven guilty. Who was she to judge? She wanted to believe that he was a trustworthy man who'd gained access to the White Star honestly and that he was a legitimate collector, but she had to know for sure.

Quickly, she googled him and learned that yes, Henri Renouf was indeed a legitimate collector who had been in business for many, many years. She scoured the information that she downloaded, looking for anything incriminating, but found nothing alarming.

Still, did she dare trust him?

Throw caution to the wind for once in your life. Take a chance.

But she'd just done that by trying to seduce Adam, and look how miserably that impulse had played out.

Yes, but her gut had told her that going to the Grand Duchess was wrong. She had acted on Cass's advice, not her own instinct. She had to ask herself this question: did she truly believe Renouf had the White Star?

In her mind's eye she could see Egmath and Batu, meeting clandestinely in the cypress grove, their love for each other eternal and pure. The story that had held her spellbound for months would not let go of her.

She couldn't help comparing the legendary lovers to her relationship. Morgan sighed with longing and cast her mind back to her courtship days with Adam.

They'd been in a study group together in college and after the group ended they just kept meeting for coffee every Thursday night. She liked him from the very beginning, their eyes meeting across the table, their smiles lingering on each other. They'd gotten the best grades in the class. Two high achievers in a mutual admiration society.

Their goals had been so closely aligned back then, their values so similar it was little wonder that they got along so well. It was breezy being with him, light and fun and hopeful. When he asked her to the symphony to hear her favorite composer she'd eagerly accepted his invitation. It turned out that they liked the same music, read the same books and enjoyed the same kind of movies.

"Cut from the same cloth," was what their friends said about them.

When she met Adam's family, his mother told her it was as if they'd just been waiting for her to walk through the door—the bond was that instant, that right. It was the same with Adam and her family. Her dad called him the son he'd never had.

The more she knew about Adam, the more she admired and respected him. He was thoughtful and gentle. He opened the car door for her, helped her on with her coat, pulled out her chair when they dined in restaurants. He bought her little gifts and never forgot important dates. He got along with her friends, and she with his. He was even-tempered and goal-oriented. And just like Morgan, he had a plan for his life and was busily on the path to success. His kisses curled her toes and when they eventually made love it felt nice and warm and safe.

Like coming home after a long journey.

Everyone thought they were the perfect match.

But it had been almost too easy. There had been no big dramas, no major conflicts to overcome, no challenges to hurdle.

Sometimes Morgan couldn't help wondering if Adam had married her simply because their relationship had been so easy. At some point had he felt trapped by the niceness of it all and drifted into the union because it was expected?

She thought quitting her job and taking on the less stressful role of shop owner would strengthen their marriage, but it had not. She'd changed, while Adam had stayed the same. Safe and nice and warm were no longer enough. In her marriage, she ached for the same kind of red hot energy, the throbbing intensity of passion that fable claimed Egmath and Batu had shared.

Weird as is seemed, Morgan felt that if she did not get to see inside that box, she would never know for sure how Adam truly felt about her. The notion was purely emotional. She knew it, yet she could not shake the irrational impulse.

For her peace of mind, she had to find out what was in that box.

Dear Monsieur Renouf, she tapped out on the keyboard. It just so happens I have plans to visit France within the following week....

IN A LAVISH VILLA IN the south of France, Henri Renouf sat back in his plush leather chair in front of his state-of-the-art computer, a sinister smile playing across his sun-weathered face.

The foolish woman had taken the bait.

She was so easy. It was like being a chess champion and condemned to play with a rabbit. But she had brought to his attention a new conquest to add to his collection, and for that he was grateful.

This new discovery of a mysterious box linked with the White Star was exhilarating and only served to fuel his obsession with the amulet and its legend of star-crossed lovers.

He had to possess that box. At all costs. He would risk everything just to get his hands on it. Nothing mattered more to him.

Renouf rubbed his palms together in a quick, excited gesture and caught a glimpse of his reflection in the mirrored tile of the wet bar across the room. He was nearly bald, and what hair he had left he vainly dyed jet-black.

Frowning, he pushed back from the chair and tramped to the mirror for a closer look. His eyes were his most striking feature—intense black pupils emphasized by remarkably clear whites. A lover had once told him that his eyes didn't seem quite human. He'd taken the comment as a compliment, not for the frightened insult the woman had intended.

Henri traced stubby fingers over the lines embedded in his forehead, the furrows running beside his nose to the corners of his mouth. They suggest experience, command, impatience with fools. But he was vain enough to hate the wrinkles and yet he loved the sun too much to stay out of it.

He had other vices, as well. Cigars and cognac and rich food. His indulgences had thickened his waist. Even so, most people thought he was in his fifties, but Henri was nearing seventy. He didn't have much time left.

He wanted the box and whatever Henri wanted, Henri got. And he didn't care who had to die in the process. He'd killed before and, if necessary, he would kill again.

Anticipation watered his mouth. It was all he could do to keep from calling up his pilot, telling him to ready the plane and jetting off to Connecticut to take the box away from the woman immediately. But he could not risk such a bold maneuver. Not when the authorities were looking for him.

But he wanted the box so badly because it represented what he'd never been able to have in real life— true love—that it was almost worth the gamble.

Patience, he cautioned himself. *Patience.*

Knowing when to attack and when to wait in ambush was what had earned him his privileged life. He would wait. Lure her in. She must come to him, on his turf.

And then he would strike.

3

ADAM SAT IN THE BACKSEAT of the mustard-yellow cab, clutching a bouquet of wilting flowers he'd bought at an all-night grocer's outside the Grand Duchess. Given that it was two o'clock in the morning, the bedraggled combination of roses, daisies, carnations and baby's breath was the best he had to offer. And he wasn't happy about it.

The taxi driver pulled to a stop outside his home on Rosemont Circle. Adam paid the fare and got out, swaying a little in the darkness. He had matched Jacobbi scotch for scotch, keeping up with his client in order to seal their new deal.

As the taxi pulled away from the curb, Adam stared up at his house.

The place was everything he'd ever dreamed of when he was a boy. A rambling four-bedroom perched stately on a two-acre lot kept well manicured by a team of pricey landscapers. In their garage sat a late-model top-of-the-line BMW, and stored at the local marina was his latest toy, Plentiful Bounty, a sleek eighteen-foot catamaran that he'd only taken out once.

He was a lucky man and he knew it, but at the back of his mind he couldn't help thinking that it wasn't enough. That he needed more. That Morgan needed more. He would simply have to work harder. She deserved the very best he could give her.

Staring at the house, thinking of how he fell short as a man, Adam realized he couldn't remember a time when he wasn't measuring his intrinsic value in terms of something tangible that other people could see.

There was the used Corvette he'd bought himself when he was seventeen with money earned working two jobs after school and on weekends. With his own hands he'd lovingly restored the car to pristine condition.

Then he had sold it at a huge profit, bought a run-down shack in a neighborhood on the verge of urban renewal in his hometown of Columbus, Ohio. He'd repaired it, flipped it and used that money to pay his parents back for putting him through college.

He was always pushing himself to do better, go higher and achieve more. It came in part, he recognized, from having parents who encouraged their four children to reach for the stars. His oldest sister, Meredith, was a renowned pediatric specialist. Of his two younger sisters, Yvonne was a concert pianist who'd played Carnegie Hall, and Brittany, at age twenty-five, was a mathematical genius on the fast track to a Nobel prize in physics.

Other than that, he'd had a conventional middle-class upbringing, where there had been a lot of talk about love but not much physical contact. He simply didn't come from a family of huggers and touchers. Achieving became like a horse race, with a limited amount of recognition for him as being special or different from everyone else in the family.

Adam focused on what he could accomplish, because if he didn't, if he ever got mentally quiet, even for a little bit, the nagging doubts began whispering. *You're not working hard enough. You're just skating by. You've got everyone fooled. You're a fraud, a fake, a poser. You're worthless.*

A sudden feeling of bleakness washed over him, surprising Adam with the sharpness of its pang. He shook his head. *Snap out of it.*

Clutching the flowers, he concentrated on negotiating his way up the flagstone path. The autumn night breeze blew cool against his face. He thought of Morgan and how good she'd looked in that sexy little outfit and how much he'd wanted to kiss her right in front of everyone at the Grand Duchess. But he was not the kind of guy who acted on such impulses. He'd spent a lifetime perfecting his image. Unfortunately, what served him well in his public life was the very thing that seemed to trip him up in private.

Tonight his wife had made a bold and daring gesture, communicating to him quite concretely what she desired. And he had let her down. He was home to make amends and he intended on spending the rest of the night showing her exactly how much she meant to him.

He pulled his key chain from his pocket and punched the button that sent the garage door rolling up. The BMW sat in one corner, a gathering of Morgan's antiques that she was waiting for him to help her haul over to her shop crouched in the other. The overhead light was burned out. Another task he'd been putting off.

Squinting at the unfamiliar shapes skulking in the shadows, Adam weaved his way toward the entryway. His head felt like the green fuzz on outdated refrigerator leftovers, and his stomach rumbled uneasily.

Swear to God, I'm never drinking another scotch as long as I live.

In the darkness, his shin clipped something.

Pain shot up his leg.

Swearing loudly, he jerked his knee up reflexively. The motion caused him to knock his foot into what he thought might be a sideboard—or it could have been a highboy. He wasn't real clear on the difference, although Morgan had tried to explain it to him several times.

Either way, it hurt like hell.

He let loose with another string of oaths as he lost his balance completely and fell backward into a grouping of dining room chairs. Amidst the screeching of wooden chair legs being propelled across the cement floor, Adam found himself lying flat on his butt, his head spinning.

Dammit, he should have changed that bulb a week ago when Morgan told him it was out.

At that moment, the side door that led into the house jerked open. Adam blinked at the sudden invasion of light and saw his wife standing in the doorway. Her face was grim and she was wielding his softball bat.

Belatedly he realized he hadn't told her he'd decided to come home.

Her chin was clenched, fingers curled around the bat, eyes narrowed in a rob-my-house-and-you-die glare. She looked darned tough with the bat cocked over her shoulder, ready to grand slam his head.

She was fierce, his Morgan. She'd defend to the death what was hers.

That's my girl.

Adam's heart swelled with pride. Tough yet so delicate you would never suspect she had an inner core of pure iron. If he were stranded on a deserted island, she would always be the one person he wanted with him.

"Adam? Is that you?"

"Honey, I'm home," he said a bit sheepishly.

"You're drunk," she said, her eyes widening in surprise.

"Just a little bit," he slurred. Adam could count on one hand the number of times he'd been drunk during their ten years together. "Jacobbi and his scotches."

She glanced at the overturned furniture. "Why didn't you come in through the back door?"

"I forgot you had the garage booby-trapped with antiques. Are you still planning on beaning me with the Louisville Slugger?"

"What? Oh," Morgan said and lowered the bat.

"Not saying I don't deserve it. I acted like an ass tonight."

Cocking her head, she studied him as if she wanted to agree, but after a couple of seconds she said, "You didn't act like an ass. It was inappropriate for me to show up dressed like that while you were trying to conduct business."

"You just caught me off guard," he said, ignoring the throbbing in his knee.

"That was the point. Spice things up. Do the un-expected."

"My mind was focused on business, and it's hard for me to shift gears, that's all. But you looked so damn hot in those sexy boots. I about swallowed my tongue when I looked up and saw you."

"Really?" she whispered. She sounded happy.

Adam was startled to realize how long it had been since she'd sounded that way. "You have no idea what you do to me."

"But you seemed mad."

"On the contrary, I was very horny."

"Oh, Adam."

"Why didn't you mention it sooner?"

"I don't know." She shook her head. "I guess I was afraid."

"Afraid of what?"

"That you weren't attracted to me anymore."

She ducked her head and looked so darn vulnerable that his chest muscles became a tourniquet squeezing off his air. He hated to think that he had made her feel as if he wasn't attracted to her.

"Aw, sweetheart, don't ever be afraid of that. I mean, look at you, Morgan. You're stunning. Any guy would give his right arm to be with you."

He raked his gaze over her. She'd changed clothes, ditching the sexy outfit for her normal pajamas. He was sorry to see the micromini go, but she still looked very hot.

"I've never felt all that pretty. I mean, my mouth is a little crooked and my chin is too firm and I'm too skinny and…"

"And I find you stunningly captivating, idiosyncrasies and all."

"Thank you for saying that."

"It's the truth."

She gazed at him with hope and longing. "I do appreciate you saying it—I know it seems silly to men, but it's important for a woman to hear."

"The flowers are for you." He extended the bouquet toward her. "I know they don't look like much, but I wanted you to know that I'm sorry for not inviting you to stay at the hotel with me."

Morgan accepted the flowers with a quick, gentle smile and lifted the droopy bouquet to her nose. "They smell wonderful, Adam. Thank you."

He could tell she'd already forgiven him and his spirits lifted. He stared into her treacle-brown eyes and suddenly felt so full of emotion he couldn't speak.

Something deep inside him whispered, *Don't ever let her go.*

"Come on, let's get you to bed," she said in a gentle

voice that went straight to his bones and she reached out to help him up off the floor.

Adam took his wife's hand.

Backlit by the light spilling in from the living room, her blond hair tumbling over her shoulders, Morgan looked more beautiful than she had on their wedding day.

Love for her smashed into his heart, splintering headlong into fragile shards of exquisite tenderness.

There were so many things he wanted to say to her, but he had no idea how to start. He wanted to tell her how much he loved her, how much she meant to him, how his world would no longer spin if she wasn't in it.

But the words clotted in his throat.

He wasn't very good at admitting his weaknesses. Never had been. He was a strong guy. He bounced back from adversity. The tender stuff didn't come easy. It wasn't that he didn't feel it. He just didn't know how to express himself in that way. It was easier to skim by on the surface, say the right things, do what was expected and look good without digging too deep, exposing too much of himself.

She's your wife. What's wrong with you? You're supposed to be able to tell her anything.

Morgan was looking at him with meticulous tenderness, and he couldn't stand not holding her for one second longer. He tugged her into the curve of his arm, pulling her up tight against his chest. He felt the steady tapping of her heart against his, heard her take a deep, shuddering breath.

She grasped his hand, turned it over and swept her soft fingertips over his hard palm, pushing waves of electricity up his arm.

"You've got me in the palm of your hand, Adam Shaw," she whispered. "You always have."

He interlaced his fingers with hers and squeezed their palms together.

With their conjoined hands pressed between them, he dipped his head and melted his lips against the underside of her jaw. He'd discovered that particular erogenous zone on their wedding night, and whenever he wanted to fully charge her up, he would nibble that sweet spot.

Moaning softly, Morgan eagerly raised her chin up to give him easier access while she pressed her pelvis against his.

If his legs had felt a little sturdier, he would have picked her up and carried her to the bedroom. As it was, he took her by the hand and led her there.

Their bedroom smelled of the lavender scent she'd always favored. If it hadn't been so late, if he didn't have to go work in the morning, if he hadn't been so drunk, Adam would have lighted candles and placed them around the room and he would have put her favorite mood music on the stereo. He felt guilty then for never having the time to pamper her the way she deserved to be pampered.

Adam promised himself that things were going to change. He would do better, be a better husband.

He looked at his wife, his eyes tracing the round firmness of her chin, accentuated by the luminescent quality of her skin. Never a sun worshipper, she took good care of her complexion, slathering it nightly with mysterious creamy female potions.

She took his face between her palms and kissed him with more fire than she'd kissed him in a very long time. Her mouth was so hot and tasty.

His equilibrium shifted, whether from the scotch or the power of her kiss, he couldn't say. But he felt it, charging through his center.

Lately their lovemaking had fallen into a familiar rhythm. Nice and steady, regular as clockwork. Nothing deviating. Nothing new or exciting. That's what she'd been trying to tell him by showing up at the Grand Duchess. She needed more. She needed to feel special. She needed him to show her that he still loved her.

He'd gotten the message loud and clear. He'd been neglecting his wife. He was here. Ready and eager to make amends.

Her dark brown eyes looked almost purple in the glow of the hallway light bleeding into the bedroom, mesmerizing him with their changeable quality.

Morgan snatched him by the front of the shirt and backed him against the wall. Her aggressiveness was unexpected but welcome. He didn't mind letting her take the lead if that's what she wanted.

"Yeah, babe," he murmured. "That's it. Go ahead. Take control."

Eagerly her tongue slipped past his parted teeth. Her nimble fingers made quick work of buttons on his business shirt. She jerked the shirt off his shoulders, flung it to the floor and with a gleeful hungry noise she spread her fingers through his chest hairs.

"You are roasting me, woman," he said, "Cooking my goose with your body heat."

She laughed.

He loved it when she laughed, which she didn't do nearly often enough. He wanted to tickle her gently under the rib cage, see if he could coax more of her laughter. That brilliant, low-toned sound was like soft music rousing him from a long sleep.

He watched her nipples harden underneath the soft blue silk of her pajamas. Licking his lips, he waited for his normal masculine response to kick in.

But it did not.

Odd that he wasn't growing harder by the minute.

She kissed him again, heatedly, anxiously, and he kissed her back, focusing every ounce of his attention on what was happening between them. Trying to generate the internal steam needed to start his engine. She rubbed her breasts along his chest and made a bold growling noise low in her throat.

That's when Adam got really nervous.

"I want to feel you all over me," she cooed. "All of you. Around me, against me, inside me. I've got to have you."

"Slow down," he said, hoping she couldn't hear the

desperation creeping into his voice. This wasn't funny. Where was his erection?

She moistened the tip of an index finger with her tongue and then reached out to trail that wet finger down the length of his throat. "I don't know if I can slow down. How 'bout we speed you up?"

He wanted her and he was happy to see that she was so sexed up. Oh, yeah. He wanted to make love to her until she screamed. But there was just one tiny problem. While his mind was willing, apparently his body had been anesthetized with alcohol.

Little Adam simply was not cooperating.

Come on, get hard.

A ripple of panic blasted through him. Not this, not this, not this. Anything but this. He was too young for this.

It's the booze. Don't freak.

Alcohol had never rendered him lifeless before. But then again, he'd never downed four scotches in one night either.

Adam closed his eyes and swallowed hard as Morgan took his earlobe between her teeth. He forced himself to dredge up some wild fantasies. He imagined them making love in all kinds of places, doing bold and kinky things that they had never tried in real life, but nothing worked.

His flag was flying at half-mast.

Dammit to hell. What was wrong with him? He remembered a time when all Morgan had to do was walk into a room and he was instantly rock-hard.

No, no. It wasn't Morgan. She was sexier than she'd ever been. The longer hairstyle she'd been growing out was a super turn-on. She kept her body fit and she was the smartest woman he knew. Any man would be happy to have her in his bed, and Adam was proud she shared hers with him.

The problem was all his.

So what was going on? Why couldn't he get it up for his smoking-hot wife?

For a man who was driven by the need to succeed, this was a devastating development. He was scared. Totally terrified.

He almost confessed to her what was going on, but he just couldn't do it. What if she thought it was because he no longer found her attractive? She was having enough self-doubt over that as it was. He would not compound the problem.

His hands trembled with desire as he touched her perky, firm breasts, but his cock would not cooperate. It was his problem and he wasn't going to burden her with it. But he would not disappoint her. It had been too long since he'd seen this kind of hunger in her eyes. He wasn't taking it for granted.

She reached for his zipper, but he wrapped a hand around her wrist to stop her before she discovered his shameful secret.

"No, no," he said and smiled brightly at her, belying the fear rapping against his skull. "Tonight is all about you."

"What?" She blinked, her eyes glazed with lust.

"Let me take you somewhere you've never been," he said. "Let me spoil you."

She looked at him, surprised, but then she nodded. "Okay."

He let out a pent-up breath of relief, guided her to the bed and helped her wriggle out of her pajamas.

She was breathing hard and staring into his eyes as if he was the most wonderful thing she'd ever seen. That reverential look made him feel even lousier.

Suddenly he felt inept and unsure of himself.

Dreamily, she closed her eyes, waiting for him to deliver on his promise. He eased onto the bed from the footboard up. He lowered his head to plant kisses over her toes. She reclined against the pillows, exhaling on adorable, kittenlike purrs.

He took his time, marking a slow pilgrimage up her legs with his tongue. First kissing the pulse point at the back of one knee and then laving his mouth over the outer curve of the other. Inching upward toward her smooth, satiny thighs.

When he was almost there, she quivered and arched her back, thrusting her breasts toward the ceiling, the ivory skin pulling taut against her chest muscles. Such beautiful breasts, sleek and riveting in their economy. Her nipples were hard little pebbles, knotting tightly in the center of her breasts.

How he loved this woman.

So why don't you make more time for her?

Because there were only so many hours in the day and you had to make choices.

Your priorities are so skewed. Remember what Jacobbi said about paying big prices for success?

She murmured something and he turned his head to listen, waiting for direction, but she wasn't saying anything in particular, just emitting little sounds of pleasure.

He loved what his touch was doing to her, whisking her away on a sea of sensation. She was so responsive to everything he did. Adam's ego would have soared except for the fact that there was still nothing going on inside his pants.

But in spite of his inadequacy—or maybe even because of it—he felt tied to her in a new and different way, bound by an enigmatic force beyond time and space.

Closer, ever closer, he tiptoed his fingers up between her thighs to the secret place that lay treasured there.

She tossed her head from side to side like a restless mare searching for her stallion. "Come on, come on, take off your pants," she urged, sitting up to reach for him. "I've just got to touch you."

"Not yet," he repeated and trailed his fingertips over her smooth, taut belly. "Lie back. Relax."

She did as he asked, moaning softly, and fell back against the pillows. "That feels so good, Adam."

He skated his palm over her upper thigh, feeling it transform beneath him, going from soft to hard as her muscles contracted, shifting as if from a liquid to a solid, a lake glazing over but with something hot instead of ice.

The old surge of passion and intense love for his wife arrowed from Adam's heart into his abdomen as he remembered the first time he'd seen her naked.

They had sneaked upstairs during an end-of-semester party their economics professor had thrown at his house, inviting only his A students. The sight of her bare skin had taken his breath.

He hadn't had a lot of girlfriends before Morgan, even though women had chased him hot and heavy. His priority had been his career; there hadn't been much time for romance.

That is, until Morgan had gotten naked with him in Professor Frye's guest bedroom. That night he'd been reborn.

One thing stood out in his memory above everything else: the sound of Morgan whispering softly, "I can't believe I'm here with you…it's magic…you're magic… we're magic."

Morgan's voice had filled his entire consciousness, flooding his chest, infusing his body with the very magic of which she spoke. He had felt like the luckiest man on earth.

In that moment, Adam had known he was going to marry her.

He was touching her now as he had touched her then. As if she were the most precious commodity in the world and he'd been entrusted with her safekeeping.

"I'm wet for you," she murmured. "So wet."

"Yes, you are."

He looked her in the eyes and his heart turned over. She

was his world. But the expression on her face told him she wasn't in the mood for tenderness. She wanted passion. She wanted hard, physical sex. She wanted him inside her, but no matter how he wished it was so, he could not give her what she wanted. He could not join her.

Not tonight.

Take care of her needs and she doesn't have to know, his fragile ego whispered.

Dipping his head, he gently kissed her straining breasts, first one and then the other. She shuddered against the pressure of his mouth. He trailed his fingers over her skin and gently nibbled first one stiff nipple and then the other, just the way she liked it.

He felt every quiver of her body, every ragged breath. With excruciating slowness he moved his hand to cover the triangle of hair between her legs.

Morgan moaned her pleasure as his hand cupped her gently.

Delicately, he inserted one thick finger inside her dewy, swollen folds. His fingertip came to rest on the secret spot he knew so well.

"Oh, Adam. Oh, baby, yes."

Her feminine energy swirled up through his hand until his whole universe spun dizzily. Her stark reaction was such a powerful thing to behold. He felt awed and blown away by her responsiveness.

"Oooh." She breathed and he felt the first ripples of a building orgasm.

Seeing that she was edging toward ecstasy, Adam

adroitly vibrated his finger against her straining cleft the way he knew she loved it.

The orgasm teased her, elusive but near. He could feel it inside her. Pressing…pressing…pressing. Closer and closer. Lifting, soaring, ready to converge in an exquisite explosion.

"That's it, sweetheart," Adam cooed. "Let yourself go."

Her eyes closed.

A dark, husky cry escaped from her lips as Adam moved down the mattress, kissing her body as he went and ending his journey by pressing his mouth against her wet, moist womanhood. She tasted so incredible.

He licked her, gently suckling her veiled hood. He ached to be inside her. To feel her pulse around him. He wanted to join her, to fly to the stars with her, but he could not.

He'd been betrayed by his body.

To chase away his feelings of inadequacy, Adam channeled all his desire, all his focus, all his need to succeed into pleasing her.

She responded with a fervency that shook him. Where had this passion come from? She rode his attention. Rode it hard and fast and full. He watched her, felt her, loved her.

And his heart split with a deep, abiding loneliness.

As his wife came in his arms, shattering breathlessly into a million pieces, for the very first time in ten years Adam Shaw feared his marriage was in serious trouble.

4

"SO HOW'D IT GO WITH Adam last night?" Cass asked the minute she breezed into Morgan's antique shop the following day at lunchtime.

"And what are you doing here?" Morgan asked, puzzled to see her younger sister in Fairfield. "Don't you have to work today?" Cass was a public relations specialist for Isaac Vincent, one of the top fashion designers in Manhattan.

"I have a charity fashion show out here this afternoon and I thought I'd drop in to surprise you." Cass carried two tall plastic glasses with lids and she had a white paper bag tucked under her arm. "So satisfy my curiosity. Did the outfit I gave you singe Adam's eyeballs?"

"What have you got there?" Morgan asked, eyeing the bag and purposely ignoring the question, teasing her sister with the suspense.

"Raspberry iced teas and cheeseburgers from Wynn's." Cass waggled the sack temptingly.

"That's so not on my diet, but they do smell good," Morgan said.

"I know a Wynn's cheeseburger is your favorite." Cass gave her an evil grin.

Morgan grabbed for the bag, but she danced out of her reach.

"Quid pro quo, my dear sister," Cass said. "You want lunch, you must reveal all."

"A lady never kisses and tells."

"I've got French fries, too. Crinkle-cut. The kind you love best."

"You're an evil woman, you know that?"

"Come on, I share all my juicy details."

"And I'm not sure Sam would appreciate knowing exactly how much you do share."

"Sam accepts me for who I really am. Impulsive blabbermouth and all." Cass sucked on the straw of her raspberry tea. "Mmm, tastes so good. Sweet and tangy, loaded with lemon and brain-boosting caffeine. You know you want one. Come on, toss me some crumbs. I'm dying to know what happened."

Morgan ducked her head, trying hard to suppress the grin that had been flashing on and off her face all morning. Last night had been truly special, and she wasn't sure she wanted to defuse the magic by talking about it with Cass. Last night for the first time in months she'd had an orgasm.

Her face heated. Correction: she'd had several orgasms. Big ones. Adam hadn't taken that much care in his lovemaking since his schedule had stretched him so thin after their move to Connecticut.

"It was over-the-moon sizzling, wasn't it? See, I told you the outfit would kill." Cass called over her shoulder to Morgan as she headed to the kitchenette at the back of the store.

At the moment, the shop was devoid of customers. Morgan trailed after her sister, delicately inhaling the enticing oniony smell of Wynn's cheeseburgers.

She shouldn't be hungry. She had hopped out of bed an hour early in order to prepare Adam a hearty western omelet for breakfast, along with hash browns and homemade biscuits. She'd even juiced her own oranges. Hot late night sex had made her ravenous. The omelet was but a distant memory in the face of the cheeseburger, but two fattening meals in one day was not a healthy choice.

Cass opened the paper bag and Morgan got a full-flavored whiff. Oh, to hell with it, she would cut back tomorrow.

"So how are the rooms at the Grand Duchess?" Cass asked, collecting paper plates and napkins from the cabinet. "Cushy?"

"We didn't stay at the Grand Duchess." Morgan swiped the other raspberry tea while Cass had her back turned.

"Hey, hey!" Cass chided, returning to the table. "That's cheating."

"Nope." Morgan took a long pull from the straw. "It's not. I told you we didn't stay at the Grand Duchess. It qualifies as information."

Cass pursed her lips in a pout and plunked down at

the table. "That info is not juicy enough to warrant raspberry iced tea."

"By the way," Morgan said, sitting beside her, "your outfit did not do its intended job. I told you Adam was different. He prefers subtle to overstated."

Cass snorted. "What do you mean? There's nothing subtle about that house of yours or his catamaran. Besides, that outfit never fails."

"It did this time." She told Cass what had happened at the Grand Duchess. How aghast Adam had looked when he'd seen her in Cass's skimpy clothing. "But then Adam came home instead of staying in the city and, Cass, I've got to tell you, it was the best sex we've had in ages."

"Did you try the technique I told you about? Making fire?" Wriggling her eyebrows suggestively, Cass took the cheeseburgers from the sack and placed them on plates. "It's one of Sam's favorites from my bag of tricks."

Morgan cupped both hands over her ears. "That's more information than I needed, thank you."

"I'm taking it you didn't try it. You gotta give making fire a shot. I promise it will drive him wild," Cass said.

"Where do you learn these things?" Morgan peeled the paper from her cheeseburger and took a bite. Heavenly.

Her sister smiled wickedly. "If I told you, I'd have to kill you. So how come you didn't use it?"

"I didn't have a chance."

"No?"

"Adam never even got naked."

"What do you mean?"

Morgan blushed.

"Oh," Cass giggled. "I get it. Adam and his trusty tongue. So guilt was what got you laid…or should we say more accurately…laved."

"Guilt? What do you mean by that?" Her sister's comment startled her.

"If Adam's conscience hadn't been bothering him about dismissing your attempts at seduction, he would have stayed in Manhattan."

"He could have just missed me."

"Then why did he focus solely on your pleasure?"

Morgan shrugged. "Maybe because it's been a long time since he made love to me in that way."

"Exactly," Cass said like a professor driving home her point.

Morgan's heart lurched. Was guilt the only reason Adam had made love to her last night? Not because she'd enflamed him with passion when she'd shown up at the Grand Duchess in her sexy outfit, but because he'd felt obligated to come home and perform his husbandly duties?

A sudden pang froze the muscles of her throat.

"It wasn't because he was hot for me," Morgan mumbled and passed Cass a napkin. "It was because he wanted to stop feeling guilty."

Shame swamped her at the idea that she'd caused Adam to feel guilty enough to come home and make love to her. She didn't want that kind of attention from him. She wanted him to want her because he couldn't stand not having her, not because she'd guilted him into sex.

"Don't obsess over it. You got laid. What's the difference?"

The difference was huge.

Morgan had awoken that morning with a smile on her face and a song in her heart. She'd felt joyous in a way she hadn't in a very long time. And now she had discovered that Adam's amorous attention was likely centered on nothing more than his need to alleviate his guilt. She felt so stupid.

The cheeseburger suddenly turned to a flavorless paste in her mouth.

This was terrible. Not at all what she was searching for. She wanted magic, dammit. She deserved magic and so did he, even though he didn't seem to realize it.

But was that dream forever out of her reach?

Don't despair. There's still the trip to France.

In a romantic environment, away from work, away from stress, they could reconnect, talk, sort things out. She just knew that they could. Because they simply had to.

Couldn't they?

BREAKFAST LAY LIKE AN anvil in Adam's stomach.

He wasn't accustomed to eating such a heavy morning meal, but that wasn't the reason he felt so leaden. He couldn't stop thinking about last night and his failure as a man.

It gnawed at him.

Nothing like this had ever happened to him and he

was worried. Not just about his performance as a man but as a husband.

He felt like a fraud. He represented himself both to the world and his wife as a person who had his act together.

But he did not.

Matter at hand, buddy. Just deal with the matter at hand.

Scowling at the papers on his desk, he restlessly drummed a pen against his chin. He tried to concentrate on the work in front of him, but it was no use. In his head he kept replaying last night like a bad movie.

How hot Morgan had looked. How turned-on she had been. And how useless and unresponsive his own body had been. He felt lost and alone.

He had wanted to talk to Morgan about his problem, but he simply hadn't known how to begin. What was a guy supposed to say? *Uh, honey, know that swell time you had last night? Well, guess what? You were in it alone. I couldn't get it up, so I pretended the night was all about you. Pretty selfish of me, huh?*

Besides, this morning Morgan had looked so damn happy he didn't have the heart to bring it up. She'd giggled and teased with him in a way she hadn't done since they were first married. He'd awakened to the smell of fresh baking and the sound of Morgan humming sweetly. She never hummed. She wasn't that carefree. Last night had been good for her, and she didn't need the burden of hearing about his equipment failure.

So Adam had zipped his lips and stuffed his unhappiness down deep inside until he barely felt it.

Well, except for the chunk of granite in his belly.

Cursing, he slammed a fist against his desk.

A colleague passing by his open door stopped and looked in at him. "You okay, Adam? You've been in here mumbling to yourself all morning."

Adam flashed him his high-school-quarterback smile. "Numbers not crunching on the Jacobbi prospectus."

"Gotcha." His office mate nodded and continued down the corridor.

What if last night wasn't a freak occurrence? whispered an ugly voice in the back of his head. *What if too much scotch wasn't to blame for your difficulty? What if there was something seriously wrong with either you or your marriage?*

Or both?

He had to do something to alleviate his anxiety. He had to focus. Had to get this promotion. It was the only thing keeping him tied together.

But how to get his mind off his sexual problem?

Romance your wife. Show her how much you really love her.

Yes, yes. That was it.

He would wine her and dine her and sweep her off her feet, just like when they were dating.

No, better scratch the wine. Alcohol had caused his problem in the first place.

Pleased with his decision, he picked up the phone and

made three calls. One to Tiffany's, one to their florist and one to the cozy Italian restaurant in their neighborhood to make dinner reservations. Tonight he was pulling out all the stops.

And what if you still can't get it up?

Adam gulped. That wasn't going to happen. He wouldn't allow himself to think that way. Everything would be all right.

"Mr. Shaw?"

He looked up from the mass of paperwork scattered across his desk to see Marcie Hopkins, the assistant he shared with three other investment bankers, standing in front of his desk. Soon, very soon, when he snagged the VP position, he could have a corner office and an assistant of his very own.

Not if you don't straighten things up with Morgan you won't.

Give me a break, he told that nagging voice in the back of his head. *I'm doing the best that I can.*

"Yes, Marcie?"

"Mr. Davidson wants to see all the department managers in the conference room."

"What time?"

"Right away."

This didn't sound good. Marcie turned and went on to deliver her message. Adam got up, took his suit jacket from the back of his chair and slipped it on. He straightened his tie, ran a comb through his hair and then joined the pack of coworkers headed for the conference room.

Speculation about the impromptu meeting was rampant, but Adam did not join in the conversation. Idle conjecture served no purpose except to whip up emotions, and he was all about keeping rampant emotions in check. Nothing good ever came of revealing one's insecurities. Perceiving, behaving, becoming. Fake it until you make it. Early to bed, early to rise, work like hell and advertise. Good mottoes that had served him well.

And he'd learned his lessons well, maybe too well. He didn't know what to do with himself when he wasn't in constant pursuit of a goal.

The minute that Paul Davidson, CEO of Criterion Bank and Trust, entered the packed conference room, everyone fell silent. The older man took his place at the podium positioned at the head of the conference table.

Davidson cleared his throat. The gathered employees hung on the silence, waiting, breaths bated.

"We've got a major battle ahead of us taking Jacobbi public," Davidson said.

Adam sat fully alert, his chest clenching with the strangling cramp of dread.

"As you know, Jacobbi Enterprises has stretched their working capital to the maximum in the course of developing their revolutionary alternative fuel source. The very thing that makes them worth taking public is what's strapped them for cash." Davidson paused as he glanced around the room at his team.

Adam knew what was coming next and he felt the screws tighten. Normally he lived for high-wire acts like this, but not now, not today, not when he was so distracted with his personal problems.

"As you also know," Davidson continued, "Jacobbi's major lender owns a large chunk of stock in the company. They've run the numbers, realize they've got a lot to lose if he goes public at this time. They've issued an ultimatum. If he proceeds, they're pulling the plug on his funding."

The bottom dropped out. Adam felt it fall away like thin ice under razor-sharp skates.

If Jacobbi's prime lender wouldn't support his bid to go public, that meant either the deal was off and Adam's chance for promotion was over or Criterion would have to find him another lender.

"I've spoken to Jacobbi," Davidson continued. "He's determined to go public, so you know what that means."

Immediately Adam's mind leaped to the task, churning frantically as he explored the options, considering possible lenders. Who else had the capital and the inclination to back Jacobbi?

"We're going to need all hands on deck for this one, people," Davidson said. "As of today, all personal leave is canceled."

A collective groan went up from the group, even though they should have seen it coming.

"For how long?" someone braved.

"Indefinitely. And you know I'm expecting us all to work eighteen-hour days to make this happen."

Reality delivered a roundhouse kick to Adam's throat. He hated to do it, but he had no choice. He raised a hand.

"Yes, Shaw, what is it?"

"Does this include vacation time, sir?"

"*All* personal leave, I'm afraid."

Adam shifted uncomfortably. Under ordinary circumstances, he would have readily accepted Davidson's edict without a quibble. Hell, under ordinary circumstances he would consider the crisis an opportunity to stand out from the pack, give two hundred percent to the project. After all, he was on the Jacobbi account. But considering his current situation at home, these weren't ordinary circumstances.

Following the meeting, he cornered his boss as everyone else filed from the room.

"Mr. Davidson—Paul," he said, praying that his boss would understand. "Morgan has already booked a two-week vacation in France for our tenth wedding anniversary. She's been looking forward to it for months."

Davidson cast him a glance loaded with meaning. "Adam, you're my go-to guy. We can't pull this off without you. I'm sorry to interrupt your second honeymoon, but this has to happen. When this is over, I'll give you an extra week of comp time. I'm sure Morgan will understand."

Ha. Little did he know. "But, sir—"

"You make this happen, Adam." Davidson's eyes never left his. "You find Jacobbi another major lender and you are my new VP. Please, don't disappointment me. I'm counting on you. Are you in? Or are you leaving me high and dry for a trip to France?"

Adam had waited so long for this opportunity. He'd spent his life preparing, planning and working hard for this moment. Everything he'd ever wanted in his career lay within the palm of his hand, and all he had to do to claim it was make a fist and hold on tight.

But would Morgan understand?

Feeling as if he were trying to clean up spilled milk with a garden rake, Adam inhaled deeply.

"I'm in," he said.

THE BOUQUET OF LAVENDER and violets took Morgan's breath away. They were so beautiful.

After tipping the delivery boy, she settled the crystal vase on the antique sideboard in the middle of the shop so she could see them no matter what corner of the room she was in. She opened the small white envelope nestled among the sweet-smelling blossoms.

Meet me at Saltori's at seven-thirty and wear what you had on last night. Love, Adam.

Morgan's heart melted along with the doubt Cass's visit had stirred up. Love for her husband filled her up and tears of happiness misted her eyes.

Everything really was going to be all right between them. And what a wonderful prelude to their vacation he had set up. A romantic impromptu dinner.

Feeling lighthearted, almost giddy, Morgan ended

up closing the shop half an hour early. She hurried home with the flowers, eager to start the evening.

She ran a hot bath, adding lavender bath salts to the water, and placed the flower bouquet on the bathroom counter, where she could gaze at them as she bathed.

Adam was such a sweetheart.

Her bridal bouquet had been comprised of violets and orchids and lavender. While orchids were supremely elegant and lavender softly soothing, it was the violets that spoke to her in a way no other flower did.

Violets smelled like singed brown sugar soaked in citrus and suede. She'd once read that violets resisted distillation and that while it was possible to concoct a high-quality perfume from the rich flower, it was exceedingly tedious and costly.

Violets were flirtatious flowers, assailing the senses with a shower of perfume one minute and the next minute leaving the air chaste, only to rouse later in a rampage of scent. Materializing, vanishing, materializing and vanishing. Playing a delicious peekaboo, elusive as a coy ingenue.

Morgan pinned her hair up on her head, got undressed and then sank into the bathtub. Steam curled tendrils of hair around her face and baked the humid scent of lavender and violets as they married in a heady romantic scent.

She lay back, contentedly propping her head on an inflatable bath pillow. Closing her eyes, she luxuriated in the moment.

Unbidden, a delicious erotic fantasy overtook her.

Against the backs of her eyelids she saw Adam, her dear husband of ten years. But in this daydream he was as mysterious to her as a stranger. He studied her with his sultry eyes. Even in his mid-thirties, he still possessed the sleekest, most buff body ever bestowed by Mother Nature, and the sight of him consumed her.

"Morgan," he whispered her name in a sultry, velvet-smooth voice that set her spine to shivering. His eyes sparkled mischievously and he flashed her a sexy-as-sin smile.

Her heart slammed against her chest at the thought of her fantasy Adam stepping cockily into the bathtub with her. Her nipples hardened and her breasts swelled. Heat pooled deep inside her.

She licked her lips and imagined what was going to happen when she and Adam got home from the restaurant. She turned a variety of games over in her head, toying with various scenarios.

She envisioned him spearing her up against the wall, his mouth ravenously taking hers as he drove himself up inside of her. Then she pictured him as a lusty pirate having his way with her, an accommodating serving wench. In her mind's eye she went from princess to prostitute to pupil, while she cast Adam first as a pauper, then as a pimp and then a professor. She giggled. So this was what Cass had been talking about. Fantasies could be a fun preliminary to the real thing.

The sweet moan escaping her lips shocked her as her imagination ran wild. She'd never known she could get so worked up over fantasies.

The heaviness in her body was another surprise.

Her own warmth was wetter than the hot bath in which she soaked. She closed her eyes, and Adam's face flashed lightning-fast against her retina like a photographer's shoot.

Click.

Whirl.

Freeze-frame.

Adam's hands, broad and flat, caressed her skin. But they weren't the smooth palms of an executive banker, rather they were the rough, callused hands of a manual laborer skimming down her throat, cupping her naked breasts, moving lower, circling her naval, teasing her mercilessly.

Another image.

This time he was a stable boy and she was a highborn mistress of the manor. There were riding crops and horses and saddles. They were in a hayloft filled with the smell of hay and leather and sex.

Their chimerical encounter was aggressive, unmistakably carnal. From where in her imagination had this sprung? He took her hard and she loved it. The only thing wrong with the scenario was that it was pretend.

But for now it would have to do.

Mewling softly, Morgan used her index finger and her thumb to lightly pinch one of her straining nipples, pantomiming what she wanted Adam to do to her.

She'd never pleasured herself before. She'd always felt too weird about touching her own body in this way. But now the thought of the unexpected thrilled her.

The game thrilled her. Touching herself and pretending it was Adam thrilled her.

She sank her teeth into her bottom lip, eyes still closed, fingers still exploring her own body. This was good. She needed to figure out exactly what she liked before she could ask him to give it to her.

Her hot spine stiffened against the cool porcelain of the claw-foot tub.

This is embarrassing, the staid part of her mind chided. *Stop it.*

No, she forcefully contradicted herself. This was empowering. This was precisely what she needed. The time and space to learn who she really was both physically and emotionally. From now on she was going to do lots of things she'd never done.

Like masturbate.

Maybe her lack of experience in interpreting her own sexual response was one of the things that had been causing problems in her marriage. Maybe this was exactly what she needed.

Resolutely Morgan caressed the naked flesh between her thighs, and all her pent-up insecurities escaped on a shattered sigh.

Adam.

She needed no anonymous fantasy lover. Her husband was the one she wanted.

Just thinking about him made her feel achy and wet and hot. She slid her fingertips over tender skin, across the silky folds, skimming along the satiny moisture oozing slowly from her swollen inner core.

"Adam," she murmured.

She pictured him in the bath with her. His caress, his hand kneading the delicate bud, dangling her on the edge of pleasure. She envisioned his mouth covering hers, his tongue nibbling, tasting, exploring. Her heart raced and her mind spun out of control.

His hand dipped between her legs, caressing, rubbing her swollen sex. He drew small circles against her inner thigh with his thumb.

Her fingers moved with the fantasy.

She was in it. All the way. No turning back. Her orgasm was just inches away, beckoning her onward.

Come.

Faster and faster her fingers strummed, adding more pressure, taking her more quickly toward her goal. Release. Relief.

She gasped at the sensation. It felt so great. Why had she never done this before?

"Adam, Adam, Adam," she cried, thrashing about in the bath, the hot water now tepid, but she didn't care. She was burning up from the inside out.

In her mind's eye she saw her husband, looking at her with the most hungry eyes, posed over the tub. His manhood, thick and swollen with desire, pushing in through her wet flesh, sliding into her innermost cave, dilating her, taking her, claiming her.

The orgasm ripped through her. Legs stiffening, Morgan arched her hips and cried out, gratification humming though her body.

She came hard, but it wasn't adequate. She wanted more. Her release, no matter how good, was steeped with loneliness. She felt as if she were in a vacuum, sucked empty. The fantasy could not compare to reality. She wanted him. Wanted him here. Wanted his body inside hers, not a phantom man.

Grabbing her towel on the fly, she flung herself from the tub, barely drying off before scurrying into the bedroom to get dressed.

Hands trembling, she yanked a pair of black-satin-and-red-lace G-string panties with matching push-up bra from the drawer of her bureau. She'd bought the ensemble to wear to France, but there was no law that said she couldn't break it out early. She slipped into the panties and bra and then caught a glimpse of her reflection in the full-length dressing mirror.

Was that really her? Morgan took a deep breath.

The lingerie made her look pretty damned hot, even at thirty-five, even in spite of a few minor dimples of cellulite dotting her upper thighs. She felt wickedly wild and she couldn't wait to get her hands on Adam and thank him properly for the flowers.

5

"IF IT'S NOT TOO FORWARD of me to say so, you're looking very beautiful tonight, Mrs. S," said the maître d' at Saltori's as he led Morgan to the table Adam had reserved for them.

"Thank you, Joe." She willed away the flush of embarrassment creeping up her neck and tried not to notice how the other diners were staring at her, dressed up again in Cass's sexy clothes.

Joe escorted her to a darkened booth in the very back corner of the restaurant, far from prying eyes. In this section, all the booths had louvered doors on them that could be closed to shut out the rest of the world.

Very private and romantic.

Joe opened the louvered door, and Morgan stepped forward to see Adam waiting.

Her husband looked so handsome in the candlelight. He got to his feet, his smile steady and sure. His voice when he greeted her was low and mellow. "You look incredible, Morgan."

Their eyes met and she halted there on the spot.

He leaned close and gave her a lingering kiss on the lips. He smelled of his woodsy cologne, but she caught the scent of something more primitive, more sensual that lay just beneath the surface.

This was what she'd been missing. This special feeling, this whisper of the unknown, this sudden magic. Excitement touched her and spread.

Morgan sat down across from him and she heard the erotic crinkle of her black leather boots as her knees bent.

The maître d' grinned, winked at Adam and closed the louvered doors behind him.

"What brought all this on?" she whispered when she was sure Joe was out of earshot.

"I realized it had been a long time since I'd done something special for you and I want to make amends for being so consumed with work. I've been neglecting you."

She'd been waiting so long to hear him say this. "Adam," she said and her chest constricted. She'd been so silly to ever doubt the strength of his love. "The violet bouquet was so wonderful. Thank you for remembering that violets are my favorite flower."

"How could I forget? You carried them at our wedding," he said.

"I didn't think most men noticed things like that."

"I'm not most men."

"No," she whispered. "No, you're not."

He reached across the table, extending his hands with his palms up.

She slipped her hands into his, and he squeezed her tight and held her locked in place with the power of his gaze.

"I've got something for you."

"Be careful," she teased, delighted. "I might get used to being spoiled."

He disentangled one hand from hers, reached into the pocket of his suit jacket and pulled out a long, slender Tiffany blue box.

She giggled, giddy with love for him.

"I was going to save it for later, but the time seems right." He cracked open the box to reveal a sparkling diamond-encrusted tennis bracelet.

"Oh!" She flashed back to the moment when Adam had asked her to marry him. That event had also taken place in a restaurant, and he'd actually gotten down on one knee. And when he had pulled that ring box out of his pocket, she was already saying yes before he even asked, because she'd wanted him that much. Morgan smiled through the misting of romantic tears. She'd forgotten how eager she'd been to become his wife.

"I just want to say thank you, sweetheart, for ten wonderful years of marriage." He removed the bracelet from the box, undid the clasp and then secured it around her left wrist. His touch lingered on her skin.

"It's so beautiful." She fingered the bracelet, admiring it. "I love it. Thank you."

"And I love you." Adam leaned across the table and kissed her again.

It was like a first kiss, only better, wondrously unique yet comfortingly familiar.

He teased her with his hot tongue, and a miniature explosion of delight went off in her mouth. She tasted him and he tasted her, their senses combining, their electrical impulses singing in beloved fusion. She relished the thick spread of sensation. His lips were sweet as taffy and as wet and hot as a tropical jungle.

Oh, *God, what a kiss.*

A ringing cell phone tore them apart. In unison they settled back in their seats, both reaching for their cell phones. Adam dived into his jacket pocket while Morgan pulled hers from her purse.

"Must be yours," she said and rested her cell phone on the table near the obligatory candle in a Chianti bottle.

"One of us has got to change our ringtone," he laughed. "Or get a different cell phone. We never know whose phone is ringing." He glanced at the caller ID. "I have to take this, but I won't be long."

Morgan brought four fingers up to touch her throbbing lips and tried not to be resentful that Adam was on the phone during their romantic dinner. He spoke to someone at the office for a few minutes, then hung up.

"I'm sorry for that," he apologized. "I'm officially turning it off." He made a show of switching off the phone and pocketing it. "Now where were we?"

"In the middle of a toe-curlingly fabulous kiss." She smiled.

"So we were." He grinned back at her and started to

lean across the table to kiss her again when there was a rap on the louvered door.

"Yes?" he called.

The door opened to reveal a grinning waiter with a bottle of champagne in his hand, along with two champagne flutes.

"For the happy couple," he said. "Compliments of the house."

"Complimentary champagne?" Morgan whispered to Adam once the waiter had poured them their champagne, taken their food order and departed.

"I told Joe that we were celebrating our tenth anniversary."

"What a great idea, starting our celebration a few days early." Morgan took a sip of the excellent champagne, felt the tiny bubbles rush to her head. "Can you believe it, in four days we'll be in Paris and then from there on to the Loire Valley. I'm so excited. I can't wait."

Adam cleared his throat, lost his smile and shifted uncomfortably in the seat across from her.

Morgan narrowed her eyes. "What's wrong?"

"Um, there's something I need to speak to you about," he said.

"Uh-huh?" Morgan struggled to smile sweetly, trying to make everything all right, but before her husband even got the words out she knew what he was going to say. She knew him so well.

He reached across the table for her again and she rested her hands in his, but this time with growing trepidation.

Adam looked her squarely in the eyes. "About our trip."

"Yes." She felt it slipping away. Her euphoria, her hope, her fantasies. Adam seemed to be slipping away before her eyes, growing grainier, less crisp. Or maybe it was just the tears pushing against the back of her eyelids. She bit down on the inside of her cheek, a trick she used when struggling to hold on to her emotions.

Adam inhaled sharply and then slowly blew out his breath. "I don't know how to start."

"Go ahead and just say it." She hadn't meant to sound so snappy, but there it was.

His hands tightened around hers. "I'm sorry, sweetheart, but I just can't go to France."

"What did you say?" She'd heard him correctly the first time, but she just couldn't believe it. Same old song and dance. She'd heard it but prayed her ears were deceiving her. This couldn't be happening. Not again.

"I'm so sorry, but there's a major snafu on the Jacobbi account and Davidson's canceled all of upper management's personal leave time." Quickly he went into detail about the problem with Jacobbi's financing.

But she didn't care. Morgan sat unmoving as a river of unexpressed emotions flowed over her. Disbelief, disappointment, regret and anger. She steeped in her anger but said nothing, did nothing. She was a master at tamping down her feelings, but being able to control her emotions didn't stop her from hurting. In fact, she often wondered if holding back made her feel worse.

This man is my husband. I chose him for better or worse. He is who he is. She told herself this, but it did not help.

"Aren't you going to say anything?" he asked.

You mean like, Go to hell?

Pressing her lips into a thin, firm line, Morgan struggled to compose her thoughts so she could speak rationally.

Adam's hands were still wrapped around hers and his eyes were on her face, but she could not look at him. She stared at her champagne, at the gay, celebratory bubbles effervescing in the glass.

She wanted to scream, she wanted to throw champagne in his face, but of course she would do none of that. She was refined, civilized. She would be a good girl and do what was expected of her, just as she'd been taught.

"I see," she said at last.

She felt as if she were a ghost, standing outside herself, watching the conversation unfold from a cold and distant vantage point.

"I'm so sorry, Morgan. I tried to reason with Davidson. I told him about our tenth-anniversary trip and he offered to give me an extra week off after this was over."

"I don't want an extra week later, I want you in France on our anniversary."

"I know, babe, but Davidson can't pull it off without me."

She felt a tearing inside her as she mentally pulled away from him, mentally stowed her heart in deep freeze.

"Go ahead and lie to yourself all you want, Adam, I know the truth."

"The truth?" He looked honestly befuddled. Was he that clueless to his own internal agenda? Had he been bedazzling so many people with bullshit for so long that in the end he had hoodwinked himself? "What do you mean?"

"This isn't about Davidson. This is about your need to achieve at all cost. Look at you." She waved her hand at his tailored suit and wrinkled her nose. "Perfectly pressed. Not a hair out of place. You package yourself as a commodity. You *are* Criterion Bank and Trust and Davidson loves taking advantage of your devotion. I wish I could inspire one third of the loyalty you lavish on that company."

"What's so wrong with looking the part? I thought you liked a well-groomed man."

"Well-groomed, yes. Flawless, no. You're like a frickin' Stepford banker, Adam."

"You used to be the same way yourself," he said softly.

"You're right," she replied. "But I've changed. I've come to see what a narrow life I was living. Do you realize that the more insecure you feel, the better groomed you get? You're determined to protect that glossy Wall Street image at all costs."

"Again, what's so wrong with that? It got us our dream house in Connecticut and it allowed you to quit your job and open your own business."

"And," she said, "it's swallowed you up. You have no idea who you really are inside. And if you don't know yourself, how can you ever know me? Adam, I—" Her voice snapped off, and at last her emotions could not be held at bay and they claimed her. Anger and sadness, loneliness and disappointment.

Her gaze fixed on the tennis bracelet.

A bribe. It had all been a bribe. The violets, the romantic dinner, the Tiffany jewelry. He'd given her those things not as gifts from his heart but as a way to assuage his conscience for choosing his career over her yet again.

She tried to jerk her hands from his grip, but he held on tight.

"I know you're upset," he said. "I'm upset, too. It's tearing me up to have to cancel our vacation. I know how much you were looking forward to this trip."

"You know nothing." Morgan raised her eyes to meet his and stabbed him with a hard glare. "Now please let go of me."

"Sweetheart—"

"Don't." She shook her head. "Don't you dare patronize me, Adam Edward Shaw."

"I'm not patronizing you, Morgan. Please, just try to understand my position."

"Let go of my hands." She made her voice icy enough to frost a cake.

Slowly, he loosened his grasp.

She jerked her hands free and with trembling fingers tried to pry open the clasp on the tennis bracelet.

"What are you doing?"

"I don't want your payoff." Dammit, why couldn't she get the stupid clasp open? *Don't you dare cry.*

"Morgan, be reasonable. This is my career we're talking about."

"No," she said, raising her voice for the first time. "This is our marriage we're talking about. You don't seem to realize that we're on the verge of losing everything and that this trip might be the only thing that can save us."

"Don't you think that's a little melodramatic?"

"No, I do not. I think it's scarily accurate." She finally wrenched open the clasp and let the bracelet fall to the table.

"When did we start drifting apart?" he asked and for the first time she saw true concern in his eyes. He knew too that things weren't as good as they should be.

"I wish I had an answer for that. Somehow we let our marriage take a back seat to work."

"My work is who I am, Morgan. You ask me to change that and you ask me to change who I am."

"Yeah," she said. "There's the rub."

She'd been dreaming of forging a magical soul-mate connection with her husband, and a dream was all it would ever be. She couldn't compete with his career. Obviously his work meant more to him than she ever would.

And the hell of it was she wasn't upset with Adam. Not really. He'd never pretended to be anything more than he was. He'd never hidden his ambitions. She was the one who wanted more than he could give. While leaving her corporate job might have set her free from the trap of constant ambition, it had left her with unrealistic hopes that Adam would someday come to the same conclusion.

This was her fault. She'd been spending too much time romanticizing the legend of Egmath and Batu. She should be happy with what she had. A husband who didn't cheat on her. A good man, a good provider. He didn't drink too much, he didn't gamble.

Why couldn't it be enough?

Knees wobbling, she scooted from the booth.

"Morgan? Sweetheart? Where are you going?" Adam's voice sounded strained with worry, but she did not look back.

She clutched her purse against her chest. She had to get away before she said something she could never take back. Something she might regret forever.

THAT HAD GONE DOWN BADLY.

Adam sat woefully in the booth, staring at the hearty plates of chicken parmesan the waiter had plunked down on the table in front of him.

Morgan had a right to be upset. He had sent her the flowers, planned the meal and bought the bracelet before he'd known he would have to deliver her this bad news, but she had no way of knowing that.

Wincing, he saw how it must look from her eyes. It must seem as though he was trying to buy her off, bribe her into accepting the fact that he was putting his work ahead of their anniversary trip. Which, in essence, he was.

But honestly what choice did he have? If he lost his job, how could they pay the mortgage? How could he take care of her?

And how could he make her understand what this promotion meant to him? He'd worked so hard all his life, performing everything as close to perfect as possible. That's why he'd picked her as his wife. She was as close to perfect as a woman could get.

Performing at the top of his game had fueled Adam's life as far back as he could remember. When he was a child his father had lost all his savings after investing recklessly in the stock market. His family had been forced to drastically scale down their lifestyle. He'd watched his father torture himself over that failure, watched his mother have to go back to work to help support the family. Adam had sworn never to make the same mistake and he became driven by the need to succeed. He came to see failure as a certain kind of emotional death, like being swallowed up by a black hole of despair. Failure, that empty darkness, was to be avoided at all costs.

And yet here you are, failing at keeping your wife happy.

He thought back to the moment Morgan had told him she wanted to quit her job and open the antique shop. He recalled a second of abject panic and found himself thinking, *what will we have in common now? Is she going to find new interests without me?* But he never spoke to her about his fear because he'd seen in her eyes that this was something she truly wanted. He would have moved a mountain for her if she told him she wanted one moved.

Knowing their income was going to be reduced had spurred him to work even harder for the VP position. He was determined to give her everything she wanted and needed. He didn't understand why Morgan couldn't see how hard he was trying. The harder he worked the more dissatisfied she seemed to become. She talked about how she wanted him to slow down, to appreciate life, but in all honesty he did not know how to do that and still give her all the things she deserved.

Should he go after her? Continue to try and plead his case even though she so obviously did not wish to speak to him. But if he went after her, wouldn't that mean he was wrong? And he could not admit he was wrong to cancel the trip. A man had to do what a man had to do in order to provide for his loved ones.

"Morgan will come around," he told himself. "Everything will be fine."

She was upset and he couldn't blame her. She had every right, but Morgan was a sensible woman. Eventually she would realize he'd done the only thing he could do under the circumstances.

And in the meantime, he would give her some space. Let her blow off steam in her own way.

Yes, yes. Let her cool off. That was the thing to do.

He picked up a fork and tried to eat but couldn't

make himself chew. Finally, he admitted the evening was a disaster worthy of General Custer, paid his tab, picked the cell phone up off the table and went home, feeling lonelier than he'd ever remembered feeling.

MORGAN GOT IN THE CAR and just started driving, with no destination in mind, her heart aching. She drove in a blind blur, her brain on autopilot, paying little conscious heed to road signs or the traffic.

She let her mind drift to the past, trying to see if she could pinpoint where their marriage had gotten derailed. It had probably started when they'd both managed to snag their dream jobs after graduate school.

It began innocently enough. At first they stopped eating meals together, grabbing food whenever and wherever they could. Then they started bringing their work into the bedroom, reading over their paperwork, prepping for the next day. Sure, they had shared this, helping each other improved their job performance, but their relationship soon became all about work.

They tried to spend time together as best they could. Carving out Saturdays as their one special day. But then Adam would have to take a client golfing or Morgan would get called in to help with the budget, and the next thing they knew those special weekly dates dwindled to monthly. They told each other it was only for a little while, just until they got ahead. They made excuses and promised to change, but months had turned to years and nothing had changed until

Morgan quit her job. But things had changed only for her, not for Adam.

Probably that was where they'd gone wrong. In the very beginning when they'd allowed themselves to get away with putting their relationship in second place behind their jobs. She thought about the past, about her role in it and how she wanted the future to be different.

It was almost ten o'clock when she reached Manhattan, and until then she hadn't realized she was headed toward her sister's apartment in Tribeca for a little tea and sympathy.

It wasn't until she was outside Cass's building that she thought about Sam. What if he was staying over with her sister?

Morgan didn't want to interrupt them if they were still in the throes of the bright glow of romantic love.

A pang shot through her heart. Would she ever feel that special glow again? That drenching soaked madly-in-love feeling. Had she ever really felt it the way Cass did, all glowing and giddy?

And the answer she came up with was no.

She remembered feeling content and safe and serene but she could recall no mad reckless desire. She had to ask herself if the easiness of her courtship with Adam was at the core of her restlessness. She felt as if he'd never had to fight for her, as if she would never know the true depth of his love for her until it had been put to test.

She thought of all the changes she'd gone through in the past year, moving from a corporate go-getter to entrepreneur. It had been tough and it had taken a lot of courage but it had been worth the effort. She made decisions differently now, than she did back then. Now, she asked herself "what will make me happy?" instead of "what do I need to do to get ahead?" By pleasing herself, she'd found both financial success and a newfound sense of herself, of what she was capable of, and she wanted the same level of success and happiness within her marriage.

Morgan never meant to pressure Adam. She knew what he was going through, how hard he worked, how difficult his job was but she also knew that his life was out of balance. She knew how much he was missing and it hurt her heart. Before they had children together, they needed to get this sorted out.

But could they?

Sadness swamped her. She was being whiny and she knew it. She should snap out of this funk, go back to Connecticut, accept what life had given her and be grateful for what she had. But she just couldn't seem to make herself turn around and go home.

Not tonight. Not without talking to someone first. Hoping that Cass would forgive the intrusion, she pressed the buzzer.

"Who is it?" Cass answered.

"It's Morgan. Would you mind if I come up for a minute?"

"Thank God you're here," Cass said. "I'm in over my head."

Hmm, what did she mean by that? Morgan wondered. With her sister, there was no telling. "I'm not interrupting anything with Sam, am I?"

"No, he's working swing shift for a month and he doesn't get off work until midnight. Get on up here. I need you."

She buzzed her in, and Morgan started up the stairs to her sister's fourth-floor walk-up.

Cass met her at the door, an apron tied around her waist, the smell of something burning in the air.

Morgan laughed. "What's going on here? You don't cook."

Cass grabbed her elbow and tugged her across the threshold, firmly shutting the door behind her. She sank her hands on her hips and glowered. "Laugh it up. Why didn't you warn me that love does terrible things to a woman, like wanting to turn into a gourmet chef?"

"What? And—" Morgan sniffed the air "—what's for dinner? I'm starving."

"Sam loves macaroni and cheese, so I thought I'd make him a surprise dinner when he drops by after work all tired and hungry. But dammit, I've already burned the sauce twice, and the macaroni got overcooked and soggy in the meantime. How in the world do you make that amazing macaroni and cheese that you're always lugging to family potluck dinners?"

Morgan looked around the room as if there might be spies and lowered her voice to a conspiratorial whisper.

"Freezer section," she said, then mentioned her

favorite brand of frozen macaroni and cheese. "Cook it up, put it in your own casserole dish, add some sweet paprika and a little grated cheese on top and, voilà, you're a chef."

"You cheat?" Cass screeched.

"Not cheating. Time-saver."

"You cheat!"

"Look, I used to make my own mac and cheese from scratch when Adam and I were first married. And then one day I was in a time crunch and tried the frozen kind. Adam raved for days about how it was my best batch ever. So I thought, what the hey, why go to all that trouble if he can't tell the difference."

"I can't believe Miss Perfect cheats."

"That's just it. The reports of perfection are grossly exaggerated. Sorry to disillusion you."

"Tell that to Mom and Dad. They still think of you as the model child."

"Even after I went rebel and left the corporate world? I thought they were sort of disappointed."

"They were surprised because you've always followed a conventional path, but they're not disappointed at all. They're proud of you. Your antique shop is only a year old and you're already turning a profit, plus you're able to spend more time with them. They really treasure that."

"I treasure it, too," Morgan said, her heart growing large in her chest. Having more time for her family was only another positive she'd realized. *That's all I want. For Adam and I to share this together.*

"So what am I supposed to do now?" Cass glanced woefully at the pile of dirty dishes in the sink.

"Relax, I can show you how to make the real stuff from scratch. You cook and I'll supervise while I'm washing up the dishes."

"Thank you," Cass said, looking a little less panicky. "You're an angel."

"You're welcome."

They started cooking, Morgan meting out instructions while filling the sink with warm water and dish soap. She welcomed the distraction of scrubbing the burned cheese off Cass's Pyrex pan.

When the dishes were done and the macaroni and cheese was baking in the oven, they curled up on the couch with a bottle of Pinot Noir.

"By the way, what are you doing here?" Cass slanted a glance at Morgan's outfit. "Dressed in those hoochie-mama clothes?"

"They're the clothes you lent me."

"I know that. They're serious-business clothes. Why are you here with me instead of at home making wild love to your husband? Trouble in paradise?"

Morgan sighed, took a long swallow from her glass of wine and then told Cass what had happened at Saltori's. "I can't believe Adam thought he could just buy me off. That I would rather have a Tiffany bracelet than a second honeymoon in Paris."

"Maybe you're just being too hard on him," Cass ventured. "Guys can be pretty clueless sometimes."

Her sister adored Adam, and Morgan had expected her to stick up for him. But that was a good thing, wasn't it? She owed it to Adam to try and see the issue from his point of view. Cass could play devil's advocate.

"He's always putting his career ahead of our marriage, and until now, I've always let him. Well, it's not good enough any longer. I want more."

"What if he can't give you any more than that, Morg?" Cass asked. "What if Adam's doing the very best he knows how?"

Morgan clenched her jaw and thought for a moment before speaking. "So I shouldn't expect anything more? I should just accept that I will never come first in my husband's life?"

"No, no, you're entitled to be happy, too."

"So what should I do?"

Cass lifted a shoulder. "You know I can't tell you that."

She was tried of talking about it. "Let's change the subject. Guess what? I heard back from Cate Wells, the archeologist I took the antique box to." Briefly she gave Cass a rundown on what Cate's expert had told her about the box and then went on to tell her about the e-mails she'd exchanged with Henri Renouf. "The deal is, if I don't go to France, I'll never find out what's in the box. Renouf is in poor health. He can't travel overseas. I either take the box to him or it's the end of it."

"Would that be so terrible?"

Morgan nodded. "I know this sounds dumb, but yeah, it would. I have to know what's in that box. I'll admit,

I've become overly invested in the legend, but I feel like if I don't ever find out what's in that box, I'll never know what's inside of me."

Cass cocked her head and looked at Morgan pensively. "I don't understand why, but I'll take your word for it. You're not the kind of person to act on impulse or get swept away by your emotions. Obviously opening this box is very important to you."

"Thanks, Cass."

Her sister reached over to touch her shoulder. "Maybe you should go to France alone."

"Without Adam? But we've never taken separate vacations."

"Nobody says you have to make a habit out of it. But this might be the wake-up call he needs. He'll get to spend two weeks without you, and you'll get the answer to the question that's been plaguing you ever since you found that box."

Go to France alone? The idea held enormous appeal. Why not?

"I could change my travel arrangements," Morgan mused. "Leave early. I could be on a plane to Paris by tomorrow afternoon. I need some time by myself. I could wander through Paris. Try to figure out what it is I truly want my marriage to be, what I want out of it, before meeting with Henri Renouf."

"You know, you never have really spent any time alone," Cass said. "You went from living in our parents' house to the dorm to living with Adam."

Morgan nodded. "You're right. I never got a chance to be on my own."

"I'm going to call Sam and ask for a rain check on tonight. We need some sister time. Why don't you call Adam and let him know where you are. He's got to be frantic by now."

Morgan shook her head. "Let Adam stew. He made this soup."

"That's not like you to be inconsiderate."

"Good. I'm tired of being like me. Tired of being Miss Perfect. Look where it got me."

"Perfect house, perfect job, perfect husband."

"My life isn't perfect, Cass. Not by a long shot. Remember, if I can fake macaroni and cheese, I can fake a lot of things."

"Still, you should call Adam. He'll be worried."

"I can't," Morgan said. "Don't you see? If I speak to him, he'll ask me to come home, and I'll capitulate because that's what sensible women do. And then I won't have the guts to go to Paris on my own. This window of opportunity is small. If I don't make a move now, I will never really know what might have been."

6

THE NEXT MORNING was Friday and Adam woke alone with a throbbing headache and a ripping feeling in the dead center of his chest. He looked over at Morgan's side of the bed.

Unrumpled, unslept in.

She hadn't come home.

His wife had never stayed out all night. Then again, they'd never had an argument like this. Hell, it hadn't even been a real argument. She had just left him sitting in Saltori's like an idiot, without one word of explanation for why she was walking out.

Come on. You know why she left. Morgan isn't the kind of woman to cause a public scene. That's exactly why you broke the news to her at the restaurant. You were too chicken to tell her behind closed doors. She's pissed at you, as well she should be.

But what was he supposed to do? Throw the promotion for which he'd worked ten years right out the door all because of a simple vacation?

Not a simple vacation but your tenth wedding anni-

versary. A vacation Morgan has spent months looking forward to.

Suddenly he felt sick. He pressed a hand against his stomach. Damned ulcer. It had been months since the last flare-up.

He swung his feet to the floor and put his head down between his knees. And when that didn't work, he shuffled to the bathroom, snagged a bottle of prescription medicine from the back shelf of a cabinet and managed to twist off the top even though his hands quivered.

The house was so quiet he could hear blue jays squabbling in the sycamore tree outside the bathroom window. An emptiness swept through him so strongly that he felt like slamming his fist through a wall. It was pure frustration.

Dammit, Morgan, do you have any idea what you're doing to me?

The phone rang.

He stumbled trying to run for it and stubbed his toe. Hopping on one foot, he grabbed the receiver on the third ring. "Morgan?"

"Adam, it's Cass." His normally perky sister-in-law sounded subdued.

"Where is she? Is she hurt? Has there been an accident?" His heart pounded against the nameless, displaced anxiety knotting inside him.

"Morgan's fine. Don't worry. She spent the night at my place."

"May I talk to her?"

"She's not here right now. She left early this morning."

"Is she on her way home?"

Cass took a deep breath and then delivered the blow. "She didn't tell me for sure, but I don't think she's ready to come home just yet. She's pretty upset."

"I screwed up, Cass. I know that. If you see her or talk to her, tell her I'm sorry. Tell her to call me. Tell her I miss her." He caught his breath. His stomach roiled. He sat down hard in the middle of the floor in his boxer briefs. "Tell her to come back home."

"I'll tell her, Adam."

"Cass, did she talk to you? Did she say why she didn't come home?" He knew the answer, but he didn't want to accept it. What he wanted was for Cass to tell him not to worry. That Morgan would forgive him. That he wouldn't have to change and everything would still be all right between them.

"That's something for the two of you to work out, Adam. You know I adore you, but Morgan's my sister and I just won't take sides."

"I can respect that."

"I'll try to get her to call you. I can do that."

"Thanks," Adam said and hung up.

He felt itchy all over, crawling with tension. He had to get out of the house. He had to move, had to occupy his mind. He had to get away from the emptiness before it swallowed him up.

He showered, dressed, skipped breakfast and went off to work as if nothing had happened.

What else could he do?

Once he was on the train, he plucked his cell phone from his pocket and stared at it for a long time, practicing what he was going to say. When he was finally ready, he punched Morgan's speed-dial number.

He heard a phone ringing once, twice, three times. It sounded close. He looked around expecting to see Morgan sitting on the seat behind him before he realized the ringing was coming from inside his jacket. Stuffing his hand into his pocket, he pulled out Morgan's cell phone. She'd been so upset and left in such a hurry last night she must have forgotten it on the table in the restaurant and he'd picked it up thinking that it was his.

Unwittingly, he'd been phoning himself. Talk about your metaphorical wake-up calls. He stared at the cell phone suddenly realizing how much his life had become dominated by electronic devices.

Adam had a luncheon with Jacobbi, and the whole time his client was jabbering about taking his company public, he found himself wondering where Morgan was and what she was doing.

"Where in the hell are you, Shaw?"

"Huh?" Adam looked up to see Jacobbi frowning at him and realized he'd barely eaten two bites of his meal.

"Your body might be here, but your head is a million miles away. Mind telling me what's more important than your plans for taking my company public?"

"Please excuse my inattention. It won't happen again."

Jacobbi narrowed his eyes. "Marital trouble?"

"What?" Adam was startled that Jacobbi had so accurately pegged his problem.

"Only one thing can make a man look that miserable and it's woman troubles. Do you want to talk about it? I know my track record is sketchy when it comes to love, but when you've lived with that many women you do learn a few things about them."

He shouldn't talk to Jacobbi about this. It was unprofessional. But dammit, he needed another man's opinion. He couldn't bring up the subject with his co-workers or his golfing buddies, and here was Jacobbi, offering to serve as a sounding board.

"Morgan and I had a big fight last night," he admitted. "Biggest one we've ever had."

Jacobbi waved a hand. "Don't worry. All couples fight. A little conflict keeps the spark in a marriage."

Adam exhaled. "This is different. Morgan got up and walked out on me in a restaurant over a romantic candlelight dinner—and that was after I'd just given her a tennis bracelet from Tiffany's."

"Whoa." Jacobbi held up his palms. "If a Tiffany's bracelet didn't win her over, then you are in the doghouse."

"Plus, she didn't come home last night, and I've been going crazy. If I hadn't talked to my sister-in-law this morning and found out Morgan spent the night at her place and that she's all right, I'd be haunting hospital emergency rooms."

Jacobbi winced.

"What?" Adam didn't like the look in the other man's eyes. "Why are you making that face?"

"Do you think your wife could be having an affair?"

"Morgan?" The idea was totally preposterous. He shook his head. "No."

"You positive?"

"Of course I'm positive. I know my wife. She's not the cheating kind."

"None of them are until they start feeling lonely and neglected because their man works long hours. Women need a lot of attention. Especially if they have too much time on their hands."

"Not Morgan," Adam denied, but his mind spun.

Morgan did have a lot more time on her hands since they'd moved to Connecticut. The antique shop kept her busy, yes, but not that busy. In Connecticut she was away from her friends, away from her sister. And with the commute and his push for vice president, he was spending more and more time away from home.

"Not Morgan," he reiterated.

Jacobbi shrugged. "That's what I thought about my first wife."

Could Morgan be having an affair? He would never know if she was. Was she that unhappy? Had she stopped loving him? No, it couldn't be that. He'd know if she'd stopped loving him.

Wouldn't he?

In despair, he tugged at his hair.

"Even if your wife is not having an affair, this is still

a bad sign. Her behavior has officially gone beyond the conflict stage into withdrawal," Jacobbi continued. "Not good."

"What are you talking about, Robert? You sound like a shrink."

"I've been to enough marriage counselors, I've picked up the lingo. And I've lost enough wives to know the truth of it."

"The truth of what?" he asked, feeling both irritated and concerned.

"The reality of marriage."

"I've been married ten years." Adam's agitation grew. He didn't want to hear that he was to blame for this and he wished he'd never confided in Jacobbi. "I think I know a little bit about the subject."

"Yeah? Then how did you get to this point?"

It was a legitimate question. One that Adam didn't want to answer.

"I'll tell you how," Jacobbi said, answering his own question. "Somehow you've disrupted the state of intimacy by failing to meet your wife's emotional needs. You had a fight, which is perfectly normal—healthy even. But then, instead of staying to resolve the conflict, she withdrew. Now that's a giant step in the wrong direction."

"What do you mean?" Alarm shot through him. "I meet her emotional needs."

"Apparently not. She's gone. Do you even know what her emotional needs are?"

"But I bought Morgan her dream house in Connecticut. It's what she's always wanted."

"Buying someone things doesn't constitute meeting an emotional need. Believe me, I argued with the therapist on that one until I was purple in the face."

"But I was behind her one hundred percent when she wanted to quit her job to 'follow her bliss' and open an antique store after that accounting scandal hit her firm."

"Yeah? So what have you done for her lately?"

Adam considered the question. Lately he'd been consumed with making vice president at Criterion. His relationship with Morgan had taken a backseat. "You're right. So tell me what to do. How can I fix this?"

"You got to snap her out of withdrawal and back into fighting mode. And then from there you gently lead her back to intimacy before it's too late."

"Too late for what?"

"Staying out of divorce court."

A HUNDRED TIMES OVER THE course of the morning Morgan thought about calling Adam, but she could not make herself do it. If she talked to him, if she heard his voice, she would give in and go home. She would cancel their trip because she loved him more than life itself.

But if she did that, then things would go right back to the way they'd been. This was the defining moment of their relationship. What she did next would determine whether they could forge the kind of deep connection she'd always dreamed of or if she would forever have to settle for less than the absolute best.

In the end, she knew there was only one way she could handle it.

After contacting her travel agent, she managed to get a seat on a four o'clock flight from JFK to Paris and then Morgan went home to pack.

She tried not to think about how much this was going to hurt Adam. Sometimes you had to go through something bad to appreciate what was good in your life. Problem was, she and Adam had been very lucky. They both had loving families. They'd both attended great schools, gotten good educations. They bought their dream house. They had every material thing they could want. Neither one of them had any big challenges to overcome. No major dramas or traumas in their lives.

Until now.

She dug a suitcase out from under the bed and unzipped it. Gently she tucked the antique box into the corner of her luggage and lovingly cushioned several sweaters around it for protection.

"This is for you, Egmath and Batu," she whispered. "Here's to the power of true and lasting love."

She finished packing and then went into her office to print off Henri Renouf's e-mail with his contact information on it and detailed instructions on how to get to his villa.

After sitting down in front of her computer, Morgan sent Henri one last e-mail telling him she would be arriving in France three days earlier than expected and that she would contact him to set up a meeting time as soon as she got there.

She set her bags in the foyer, telephoned for a taxi and then turned to write Adam a note explaining why she was leaving.

And that's when her husband walked in through the back door.

"MORGAN?" ADAM LOOKED from the suitcase at her feet to the overnight bag thrown across her shoulder. She was pale-faced and dry-eyed, her small chin fierce and round and determined.

"Adam."

"What's going on?"

She raised her eyes to meet his. She seemed eerily calm, looking at him as if she hardly knew him, as if she had no feelings for him one way or the other. That look scared the hell out of him.

"I'm going to France," she said.

"Alone?"

"Yes."

"Now?"

"Yes."

"But our trip doesn't start for three more days," he said.

"I've altered my travel plans, just like you altered yours."

"Morgan, sweetheart, I'm sorry." He gave her his most charming smile, but nothing doing. She was on to his bag of tricks and she wasn't falling for his let's-make-a-deal grin.

"There's nothing to be sorry for. You did what you had to do and I'm doing what I have to do." She shrugged. She wasn't giving in on this.

"Don't go." He took a step toward her.

She held up both palms. "Please don't touch me. I won't have you cajoling me out of this."

"I don't understand why you have to go."

"And I don't understand why you're not coming with me."

"My job."

"Exactly," she said. "Your job."

He felt as if there was this huge, gaping chasm stretching out between them rather than a matter of a few simple feet. He'd never felt so disconnected from her, so cut off. They stood there, not saying anything, the heaviness of the years they'd spent together rolling between them like a shifting quicksand. Adam suddenly felt exhausted.

"There's nothing I can say that will get you to stay here?"

"Nothing short of 'I'm dying.'"

"I'm dying." He made a bad attempt at joking.

"Stop it." She glared. "That's not funny."

"Morgan—"

"Listen to me," she said. "I'm doing this for both of us, Adam. I need time to think about us, this marriage, what I want."

"I need you."

"Well, I've needed you for a long time and you haven't been there for me. I mean, dammit, Adam, you can't even help me cart that furniture in the garage over to the antique store or change the burned-out light bulb."

"I'm sorry. You're right. Let's do it right now."

She just stared at him, and he felt about as useful as carpet lint. "To tell the truth, I feel like you've forsaken me."

"I haven't forsaken you." He made a dismissive noise at her dramatic choice of words.

"I didn't say you did, I just said it's the way I feel and by the way, what are you doing home so early? I didn't expect you before midnight, if then."

"I couldn't concentrate. I was miserable all night without you. I promised Davidson I'd spend the entire weekend working on Jacobbi's battle plan if I could leave early."

"So you came home to work even harder than you would have at the office." She shook her head. "And you wonder why I'm leaving on a trip without you. Hello? It doesn't even matter if I'm here or not. Your mind is always on your job. At least I might as well be enjoying myself strolling through the Louvre."

"Hey, hey," he said as it suddenly occurred to him that she'd been trying to sneak out and avoid this confrontation. "You were just going to slip off without a word to me?"

"I was going to write you a note." She had the good grace to look ashamed of herself.

Outside, at the curb, the honk of a car horn blared.

"It's my ride," she said. "I have to go."

"All right," he said. "If time alone is what you need, then I can understand that."

He reached down for her suitcase, but she wrapped her hand around it first.

"No need to walk me to the cab. I can handle it."

"You sure?" He stared at her, trying to read what was going on in her head.

"Yeah." She nodded and dropped her eyes.

"No kiss goodbye?"

"Yes, sure, of course." She stepped forward and he folded her into his embrace.

Hugging her shouldn't have felt awkward, but it did. She brushed her lips against his—quickly, without pressure or warmth—and then stepped back.

He was hit by a desperate impulse to fall down on his knees and beg her not to leave, but he did not. Losers begged. He swallowed hard.

The taxi driver honked again.

"I've gotta go." Her smile was slight, barely there.

"Wait." He laid a hand on her shoulder.

"Yes?" Her voice was whisper-soft, expectant; her eyes dark and shiny as if she were on the verge of tears.

"I've got your cell phone. We mixed them up again." He took it from his pocket and pressed it into her hands. Her skin felt cool to his touch.

"Thank you," she said.

"Have a safe flight."

"You be careful."

The taxi honked once more, this time long and insistent.

Morgan turned, suitcase in hand, and stepped out onto the porch.

I love you, he wanted to whisper as she walked away, but he could not. The words were glued to his throat, refused to come out. He was terrified that if he said them, she would not say them back to him.

And he could stand anything but that.

She stopped, turned back and smiled sadly. "Take care of yourself, Adam."

And then she was gone, down the sidewalk, swallowed up by the yellow taxicab.

He stood on the porch long after the taxi had disappeared from sight, staring helplessly at the empty street, at the neat spacing of expensive homes on his block. A dark solitude settled over his heart. He felt as if someone had just chiseled off a big chunk of his soul and tossed it into a fathomless ocean. He should have stopped her from leaving. He should have said something that would have compelled her to change her mind and stay.

Morgan had said she just needed some time alone, but Adam wasn't so sure that was the truth. Was he losing her?

If you are, no one to blame but yourself. You're the one who let her go.

Dammit, Jacobbi was right. She'd withdrawn from him all the way to France.

And then Adam remembered what else Jacobbi had said. *Do you think she could be having an affair?*

Nah, not his Morgan.

She couldn't. She wouldn't.

Would she?

He ran a hand through his hair. He had to stop thinking about this or it would eat him alive. Even if he worked nonstop all weekend he would still be behind the eight ball come Monday.

Shaking his head to clear it of any thoughts except Jacobbi's project, he rolled up his sleeves, called for pizza delivery and then carried his briefcase into his office.

He plopped down at his desk and woke his computer out of sleep mode. He took the zip disk with Jacobbi's project on it from his briefcase and plugged it into the external drive, only to discover that his disk drive wasn't functioning.

Mumbling a few curse words under his breath, he ejected the disk. He'd just have to work at Morgan's computer. He gathered up his papers and headed into her office, right across the hall from his.

She'd left her computer on, which wasn't like her. She must have been in such a rush to get out of here before he got home that she had forgotten to shut it off.

Readjusting the position of her office chair to accommodate his longer legs, Adam sat down, touched her mouse and discovered that she hadn't even logged off the Internet. She really must have been in a hurry to get away.

Gloomily he moved the mouse to click off the Internet connection when he saw the instant-messaging screen displayed on her computer. It wasn't his intention to spy or pry, but there was an e-mail message just sitting there waiting for him to read.

My dearest Morgan,
My heart beats fast with excitement just knowing you will be arriving in Paris three days earlier than planned. I can't wait for our rendezvous. Call as soon as you arrive. I'm looking forward to seeing you and that unique box of yours and discussing our mutual love of antiques.
Adieu,
Henri Renouf

Stunned, Adam read the message again and again and again.

Who was Henri Renouf?

He'd heard about Internet infidelities and virtual affairs. Was Morgan on her way to France to have a fling with someone she'd been corresponding with online? Someone with whom she could share her love of antiques?

His blood ran cold and momentary alarm brought prickling to his skin—an alarm that seeped surely, steadily into dread.

Adam slumped back in the chair feeling as if he'd been run through with a sword. If Morgan had decided to have an affair, then it was all his fault.

"She's not having an affair," he said out loud to convince himself of it.

Maybe not yet, but she's ripe for attention, and this Henri guy seems prepared to give it to her.

They'd been married ten years. He'd been neglecting her. She was restless and longing for something more. She would be in France, yearning for romance, alone with this horny Frenchman who loved antiques as much as she did.

Rage struck him. He was out of his chair, pacing the room, imagining Morgan in a hundred different romantic scenarios with this Henri character.

Angrily he ground his teeth.

What had he done, letting his wife take off for France alone?

Dull despair slapped him like a faceful of ice water. If he had stood up to Davidson and told him he was going on his anniversary trip no matter what, none of this would be happening.

And you wouldn't be getting your promotion.

No, but neither would he be on the verge of losing his wife. He simply would not let this happen.

There had to be a way around his dilemma. A way he could get his promotion and still show his wife how much he loved her. One thing was for sure: he had to win her back. He had to prove that he was the man for her and he would spend the rest of his life making sure she knew and understood that.

Think, think. Come up with a plan.

It was Friday evening. Adam glanced at his watch. If he caught the next flight to Paris, he could be there by morning, just a few hours after Morgan. They could spend two days together and then fly back home Monday morning Paris time. He'd lose sleep, but so what? He would make it to work and make his wife happy, as well.

A weekend was better than nothing. Surely once she saw that he was eager to compromise, she would be willing to meet him halfway. She would see that he did care for her more than his work.

"Morgan," he murmured. "I promise I won't forsake you. I won't drive you into the arms of another man."

But there, in the back of his head, he heard a faint scratching, like white noise on a television turned down low but not low enough. *But what if you already have?*

7

JUST AFTER SIX O'CLOCK Saturday morning Paris time, Morgan was standing near the baggage carousel at Charles de Gaulle International Airport, watching as piles of luggage spun around and around. She'd been here for almost thirty minutes and she'd yet to see her suitcase circle past.

One by one, tourists and travelers plucked up their bags and then drifted away until only Morgan was left and the carousel was empty save for a large white cardboard box tied up with yellow twine.

Her luggage was not there.

Nibbling her bottom lip in concern, she walked to the lost-luggage counter to speak with the desk clerk. He took her claim ticket and went to check the storage area. He returned a long while later, shaking his head. "It is not there," he said in heavily accented English.

"Where's my luggage?" Morgan asked.

"I will consult the computer."

The desk was crowded with other disgruntled passengers who'd lost luggage, complaining and demanding attention. Sighing, Morgan leaned her elbows on the counter.

"I am sorry to inform you, madam," the clerk said, "that your bags have been sent to Thailand."

"What?"

"Of course, the airline is extremely apologetic for the mix-up and they are doing everything they can to get your luggage returned to you as quickly as possible. In the meantime, they are willing to issue you a travel voucher for your inconvenience."

"No," Morgan said. "This can't be happening. There's something quite valuable in one of my suitcases."

He sniffed disdainfully. "Then you should have purchased additional flight insurance."

"So what am I supposed to do now?"

"You may fill out a claim." He pushed a triple-form pad toward her.

"But you don't understand. I need that item now. Today. It's important."

"Madam, I'm sorry, but there is nothing else I can do. Your luggage will be shipped to your hotel as soon as it arrives. Next time put your valuables in your carry-on bag."

Morgan stared at the claim form and a sick feeling stole over her. It was official. Her luggage, with Egmath and Batu's box inside, was missing. She huddled near the counter, arms wrapped over her chest, buffeted by the crowd—alone and vulnerable and confounded. Her fingers curled into fists of despair. The primary reason she'd left her husband was in that suitcase.

And now it was gone.

Plus, Henri Renouf was waiting with the White Star, waiting for her call, waiting to open the secret box with her.

What a fiasco.

She found a place to sit out of the direct path of airport foot traffic and dug her cell phone from her purse. She searched her address book for Henri's number and placed the call.

He answered immediately with a pleasant voice. "Henri Renouf."

"Monsieur Renouf, this is Morgan Shaw," she said in French.

"*Bonjour,* Morgan. Please call me Henri. Are you in Paris?"

"*Oui,* I have just arrived."

"*Très bon.* When can we meet?" He sounded very excited.

"I'm afraid, Henri, that there's a bit of a problem," she said.

"A problem?" he repeated, and she heard his tone switch from eager to guarded.

"Nothing to be alarmed about. It seems the airline has sent my luggage to Thailand. Unfortunately the box was inside."

"You packed a valuable antique in your checked

baggage?" he said, incriminating her with the same thought that had been kicking around in her own head.

"I know." She sighed. The only excuse she had was that she'd been so upset with Adam she hadn't been thinking straight. "It was stupid of me."

There was a long silence on the other end of the connection. Finally Renouf spoke. "If you do not have the box on your person, you do not have the box on your person. We will meet whenever you have it in your possession again."

"Thank you for understanding. The airline has assured me they've put a trace on the luggage and it will be arriving in Paris soon."

"Very good." His English was impeccable. "Call me the minute it arrives. Whatever the time."

"Anytime?"

"Day or night. I am troubled with insomnia. You won't awaken me."

"All right."

"Good day, Morgan."

"Good day, Henri." She hung up with an odd feeling, like a thorn of warning, in her throat.

She was beginning to think Henri Renouf was as obsessed with the box as she. What was it about the legend of Egmath and Batu that held such sway over people?

The power of true love, she reminded herself. There was nothing in the world so compelling.

HENRI RENOUF CALMLY hung up the phone when he wanted nothing more than to slam it savagely against the wall.

Anger burned like a hot bullet inside him, but Henri never allowed himself to lose control. Or rather, very rarely. He certainly was not going to allow some feeble-minded American housewife to cause him to lose his temper.

Folding his arms over his chest, holding his anger tight against his heart, Renouf paced the length of his study.

Had the silly woman's baggage with the antique box inside really been lost by the airline? Or was this some ploy on her part? Was she going to try and extract money from him by withholding the box?

She'd never said anything about money. But she could be feeling him out, leading up to it. He would pay a great deal for the box. His curiosity was ablaze within him, growing brighter each moment that the box was not in his possession. But that was not the issue. He would not tolerate extortion from anyone.

What was his next move? Should he give her some breathing room in case her luggage truly had been lost? Or should he fly to Paris and confront her personally?

Perhaps there was another option.

He could send one of his men after her.

But who? He'd been forced to dispose of Allard, the thief he'd commissioned to steal the White Star in the first place, and a couple of his other associates had been arrested not long ago by MI6. He couldn't send his personal bodyguard. He was fresh out of lackey thugs.

But there was Tomas Solange.

The man was an antiquities specialist and an historical scholar. He was well versed in many African languages and he was the one who had told Henri about the White Star in the first place. Who better to send on a mission to retrieve the box than the man who was living in his guesthouse while he was working on his dissertation. He owed Henri a lot.

Henri picked up the phone and called the guest cottage. Tomas answered on the tenth ring. He sounded as if he'd either been sleeping or deeply caught up in research. Henri summoned him to the house.

Tomas appeared within minutes. The man might be an intellectual wimp, but he knew where his bread was buttered.

"Yes, Mr. Renouf," Tomas asked, "what can I do for you?"

"Have Pierre drive you to the train. You're to leave for Paris immediately."

"What for?"

Henri smiled. He knew his answer would intrigue Tomas and ensure his cooperation. "To locate the box that the White Star opens."

"There's a box?" Tomas's eyes lit up.

Briefly Henri told him about Morgan Shaw and what she had found in the basement of her little antique shop in Connecticut.

"What do I have to do?" Tomas asked.

Henri surveyed him in his rumpled clothes and unshaven jaw. "Clean up. Groom yourself. Dress in that business suit I bought you. Look the part of a wealthy man. That way no one will ask questions. Go to the Hotel La Fontaine and search the American woman's hotel room. Find the box and bring it to me."

"And if it's not there?"

"Then call me. You'll stay in Paris, observing her movements. Perhaps she is telling the truth and the airline did lose her luggage, but perhaps she is not."

"Yes, sir. But what happens if she catches me in her room?" Tomas asked.

Henri smiled with all the anger in his heart. "Then kidnap her and bring her here to me."

JET-LAGGED BUT TOO keyed up over her missing luggage and the time change to sleep, Morgan lay in the middle of her bed in the honeymoon suite at the La Fontaine hotel. From her bedroom window she could see the Eiffel Tower rising up in the early-morning light.

Here she was in the honeymoon suite and no honey with which to moon.

She'd booked the perfect room in the perfect city for the perfect anniversary celebration, and look how it had turned out. Wearily she passed her hand over her eyes, burdened by lack of sleep and the ache of loneliness gnawing at her bones.

She'd dozed on the plane, but every time she had

nodded off, she'd had bad dreams that Adam had been hurt. That he'd been in an accident and she'd been unable to find her way to the hospital. He was missing and she was lost. She wandered through streets and towns, buildings and parking lots, calling his name, to no avail.

Finally, to stave off the nightmares, she'd asked the flight attendant to keep bringing her cups of strong coffee to keep her awake. Now she was wired and jittery.

Eager for a distraction, she got up and yanked the draperies closed so she wouldn't have to look at the Eiffel Tower mocking her with its romantic majesty. She picked up the remote control from the bedside table, turned on the small television set tucked discreetly in an armoire and flopped back down on the bed.

Idly she flipped through the channels, delighted to realize she understood most of what was being said on TV. Her French lessons had paid off. Unfortunately there was no Adam here to impress with her newfound skills.

She stopped flipping when she saw fur-coat-clad Omar Sharif huddled in the snow. *Dr. Zhivago.* One of her all-time favorite tearjerkers, and it was just starting. The story was so tragically sad. Just like Egmath and Batu. Soul mates unable to be together.

Morgan called room service to order a snack and then retrieved a box of tissues from the bathroom and piled back onto the bed to watch the show.

The phone rang.

She was tempted not to answer.

But what if it was Adam? Or the airline saying they'd found her luggage? Maybe it hadn't been sent to Thailand after all.

She picked the receiver up, eyes still trained on the TV. "Hello?"

"So are you by yourself? Or did Adam change his mind and go with you?" Cass asked.

"What are you doing up so late?" Morgan checked her watch and did a little mental math. "It's almost midnight your time."

"Sam doesn't get off until midnight, remember? Swing shift. So which is it? Are you alone? Or am I interrupting something magical?"

"No magic here. I'm alone." Morgan sighed. "Watching *Dr. Zhivago*."

"Say it isn't so." Cass groaned. "Not *Dr. Zhivago*. That movie makes you so hopelessly melancholy. Turn it off right now."

"I'm already hopelessly melancholy. The good Dr. Z is simply validating my dreary mood."

"I don't get why you like that movie so much. It's depressing."

"Come on, it's romantic. They love each other desperately and yet they can never have each other. All that poignant longing. All that hot chemistry. All that potential that goes unfulfilled. Just like with Egmath and Batu."

"You're sort of into that whole tortured unavailable thing, aren't you? *Romeo and Juliet* is your favorite play. *Dr. Zhivago* is your favorite movie. Egmath and Batu is your favorite legend. Don't do this to yourself."

"Don't do what?"

"You know you have a tendency to disconnect from people when you're upset. You're in a foreign country alone when you're supposed to be on your second honeymoon. That's bad enough. Don't stir the pot by watching a movie that makes you feel sad."

"You're the one who told me to come to France by myself." Morgan made no move to extinguish Omar Sharif and Julie Christie, who were gazing longingly into each other's eyes as they faced permanent separation.

"Maybe that wasn't such good advice. Not if you're going to get into a funk."

"My funk goes deeper than that. The airline lost my luggage, and the box was inside of it."

"That sucks."

"I know. I feel paralyzed without it. I mean, it's the reason I left my husband at home."

"So did you talk to Adam before you left? Does he even know you're gone?"

"He knows."

"And?"

"And nothing."

"He doesn't care?"

"Not enough to come with me."

Cass made a noise of regret. "I wish I could be there to give you a big hug."

"It's okay. I'm okay. Stop worrying and go enjoy Sam," Morgan said.

"I can't enjoy him when I know you're going through something bad."

"I'm fine."

"Are you really?"

There was a knock at the door.

"Look, Cass, I gotta go. Room service just brought my breakfast."

"I'm only a phone call away if you need me."

"I know, thanks."

"Morgan?"

"Uh-huh?"

"No matter what, I love you. Mom and Dad love you and I know that Adam loves you deeply even if he is acting like a typical male lunkhead at the moment."

"You really think so?"

"I know so."

Morgan hung up the phone, hoping against all indications to the contrary that on this issue her little sister was right.

It was just before noon on Saturday when Adam's plane touched down in Paris. The minute they were on the ground he tried Morgan's cell phone but couldn't get through.

Outside the airport he grabbed a taxi in the miserable wet drizzle to the La Fontaine. After identifying himself at the front desk as Morgan Shaw's husband and showing his ID, the desk clerk finally told him what room she was staying in.

Number 329.

Feeling more nervous than he had on their wedding day, Adam took the elevator to the third floor. What was he going to say to her when he saw her? He'd had several hours on the flight over to rehearse a speech, but now nothing sounded right.

He got off the elevator and started down the corridor. He spied a man carrying a jaunty red umbrella coming from the last room on the left.

Adam counted the numbers over the doors as he walked down the corridor. Room 321, 322, 323. The closer he got, the more he realized he was moving toward the door where the other man had just emerged wearing a smug, self-satisfied smile.

Adam's hands curled into instinctive fists. He smelled trouble.

The man passed him in the hall without even flicking a glance in his direction. Black hair and muscular, the stranger carried himself with the air of the well-bred and he wore an expensive business suit. This man wasn't part of the hotel staff. He was a guest.

Or the lover of a guest.

Adam's pulse skipped as his mind raced ahead, counting the remaining room numbers, knowing the even numbers were on the right, the odd numbers on the left. Knowing that room 329, Morgan's room, was the last one on the left. Knowing that this man had been in his wife's room.

Don't jump to conclusions.

But with the way Morgan had been behaving, it wasn't a giant leap.

He ground his teeth as he reached the last room on the left. Yes. Room 329. Anguish gripped him and he pivoted on his heel.

"Henri!" Adam shouted.

The man, who was now standing at the elevator, turned and looked at Adam over his shoulder down the long length of corridor, a startled expression on his face. He was dark, swarthy, handsome. Next to him, Adam felt bland in his Nordic blondness.

Was this him? Henri Renouf? The French bastard who'd been e-mailing his wife?

"Hey, you! Wait right there. I want to talk to you, buddy. What were you doing in my wife's room?" Adam rushed toward him, his raincoat whispering nosily as he ran, water splattering over the carpet.

The man gave him an inscrutable smile and stepped onto the elevator.

An odd kind of panic set in that he could not define, and Adam began to shiver.

No time for this. Get after him.

His feet stumbled and his knees wobbled. He dashed down the corridor, nearly falling in his haste.

The elevator doors slid closed just as Adam reached it. Viciously he punched the button, willing the door to open so he could drag Henri Renouf from the elevator car and pummel the hell out of him.

But the doors did not open.

Breathing hard, Adam plunged down the stairwell, running at top speed, determined to catch Renouf by the time he reached the lobby.

His feet hit the bottom landing with a thud and he slammed through the fire door, tumbling out into the lobby. Guests stared. He scanned the area, saw the elevator had already arrived on the ground and Henri Renouf, with his cocky red umbrella, was disappearing out the revolving door onto the street in front of the hotel.

He felt his face whiten, grow cold with anger and fear. Adam ran after him, almost knocking down an elderly woman in the process. Mumbling an apology, he dashed outside only to discover the man was lost to him, swallowed up by the gray, misty fog.

UNBEKNOWNST TO MORGAN, at the same time Adam was on his way to Paris, she was wandering the rain-soaked streets of Paris, appropriately dejected after watching *Dr. Zhivago*. She felt the day's dampness all the way to the center of her bones, but she refused to let the inclement weather stop her. She was here to evoke old memories. She was trying to resurrect what she and Adam had shared in this city of love. Trying to revive the past while she waited on the airline to find her bags so she could proceed with the next phase of her journey.

She took in the stone buildings, elegant arches, public

sculptures. She walked uneven cobblestone streets. She saw food arranged in artful piles gracing storefront windows—long loaves of thick-crusted bread, hard wheels of tawny rind cheeses, thick stacks of colorful autumn vegetables.

Her memory of her honeymoon was hazier than she thought. She remembered sauntering hand in hand with Adam through the Louvre, recalled kissing him outside a famous cathedral, recollected eating dinner with him at a cozy restaurant near the Seine. But for the life of her she could not remember how she'd felt.

Had she ever been a giddy newlywed? Surely she must have felt that sweet ache of romance, but her mind refused to dredge up the emotions.

Finally, tired of feeling soggy, she rode the Metro. She caught sight of herself in the glass. Her body appeared ephemeral cruising across the urban land-scape. She didn't recognize the woman she spied there. Who was this stranger? This woman who had left her husband behind? This antique store owner who dared a foreign country alone?

Around lunchtime the need for warmth, dryness and refreshment drove her back toward the hotel. The fog deepened near the Seine, grew so thick it was hard to make out the changing traffic lights at the intersections as she walked toward the hotel, shoulders hunched against the damp wind.

A man emerged from the mist, walking toward her.

Six feet tall, fast-paced gait, broad muscled shoulders. A thatch of wheat-colored hair.

Her chest tightened.

My man, she thought.

But that was ridiculous. This man couldn't be Adam.

She drew closer.

Could it?

But there was no mistaking the set of those quarterback shoulders. Her heart leaped with joy.

It was him!

Her man.

"Adam," she whispered his name under her breath. "You came."

She felt weird and wired and didn't know what to do. Should she throw herself in his arms? He wasn't much for public displays of affection and he looked angry, with his mouth set in a grim, unforgiving line. She'd never seen him looking so stern. He looked as if he wanted to wrap his hands around someone's neck and squeeze as hard as he could until they were dead.

Was she that someone? Morgan shivered.

Had he seen her?

Acting on instinct, she quickly glanced around, saw a narrow alleyway between two shops and darted into it.

Her heartbeat jackhammered in the hollow of her throat. She pressed her body flat against the brick wall of the building behind her, her gaze trained on the flow of foot traffic on the sidewalk beyond.

She had no idea why she was hiding from him. She

was happy that he had come to Paris. And if he was angry with her…well, that was a good thing. It meant he was ready to fight for her and for their marriage.

The only thing that kept her from stepping out of the alleyway and shouting his name on the street was the hot, heavy feeling pushing through her lower abdomen, suffusing her sex with a persistent throb.

Hiding from him turned her on.

He came into her field of vision, mingled in among the crowd. He passed so close to where she was hiding that Morgan could have reached out and grazed her knuckles over the nubby material of his tweed sport coat.

She must have sent out some kind of sexual vibe, because he stopped, turned and looked over his shoulder. Terrified yet thrilled that he would see her, she pivoted on her heel and ran down the alleyway, mouth dry, heart pounding, body tingling with a surge of adrenaline.

Had he seen her?

Would he follow?

In spite of the loudness of her blood churning through her ears, she heard the slap of footfall on cobblestones behind her.

He was coming.

Morgan grinned and slowed her pace to a quick walk.

Their game of cat and mouse had begun.

8

From his peripheral vision Adam caught sight of a woman lurking in the alleyway between a bakery and a cheese shop.

Morgan?

Adam stopped, disrupting the flow of the foot traffic, turned his head and looked behind him just in time to see the back of a woman's head as she darted away down the alley.

She was blond, lithe, dressed in sensible brown slacks and a ginger-colored jacket. He recognized the jacket. He'd bought it for her on her thirty-fifth birthday.

"Morgan?" he whispered.

The woman moved like his wife, with her no-nonsense stride and indomitable grace.

But why was she running away from him?

Maybe she's not running away from you but toward him, Henri Renouf, her lover.

Adam gritted his teeth and, without thinking his actions through, plunged down the alley after her.

She'd already reached the through street and had vanished from his view. He had to hurry to keep up with her. She could disappear on him at any moment and he would never know what she was really up to.

The air in the alley seemed to quiver with her spirited sexuality, beckoning him onward. He was making it up, he realized, creating something from nothing. The woman might not even be Morgan.

But his gut told him it was his wife. He had known her for over a decade, made love to her, woken up next to her, cared for her when she was sick. His heart recognized her.

He arrived at the through street. He was breathless not from exertion—he was in great physical shape. Rather it was fear that stole his oxygen. Fear that he would lose her. Fear that he had already lost her. He jerked his head, looking right and then left. Panic was a solid hand reaching down and fisting around him.

Where was she? Which way had she gone?

There. At the end of the block. He caught sight of the ginger-colored jacket, capped off by a cream-colored scarf, merging into the line of tourists waiting in front of the glass pyramid to get into the Louvre.

The fist clutching his insides relaxed. He would find her in the museum.

And if that's where she was going to meet her lover?

The fist tightened again.

He had to know for sure, no matter how painful the truth. He walked to the back of the ticket line. Morgan had already gone inside, and it seemed an eternity before his turn came and he was finally through the doors.

The crowd milled thickly in the entryway atrium as

people got their bearings and figured out what they wanted to see first. A large percentage of the throng headed off for the Italian Renaissance collection in search of the Mona Lisa.

Following a hunch, Adam consulted the site map and then went for the Decorative Arts section. The way Morgan had been obsessing over that damned box she had found in her antique shop, he figured she would either go in that direction or toward the Egyptian collection.

And if she's not in either of those places? What if she's meeting her lover in a secret alcove somewhere?

Adam rubbed a palm along the back of his neck, trying to silence that ugly voice that seemed to want to believe the worst.

A familiar scent of lavender caught the attention of his nose. He looked over just in time to see the ginger-colored jacket disappearing around the corner of a display case.

Did Morgan know he was following her? Was she purposely teasing him?

The thought that she'd spied him on the street and then plotted to lure him here for a delicious and unexpected seduction shot a hot wad of lust through his body.

He hurried after her, determined to find out if this was true, wanting so badly for it to be true. She had no other lover at all. This was just Morgan's attempt to snazz up their sex life.

What about the guy at the hotel?

Adam shook his head. It must have been a mistake. Either he had been on the wrong floor or the guy had not yet checked out of his room even though it had been assigned to Morgan. Mix-ups like that happened all the time. He wasn't going to think about it anymore. He was focused on what was in front of him. He was a hunter in pursuit of his sexy quarry.

Wandering through the Decorative Arts section, his eyes were on the visitors, not on the displays. He ignored pottery and glassware, bypassed ceremonial vases and funeral urns. A group of elderly tourists with a chatty tour guide eyeballed a collection of snuffboxes. Adam detoured around them, craning his neck, trying to see beyond into the next room.

No Morgan.

Dejected, he stared blankly into a glass case filled with music boxes, and that's when he saw her reflection. Alluringly she winked.

Adam spun around, but she had disappeared on him again, slipping into yet another room.

His grin widened. No question about it. The game was on.

MORGAN HID BEHIND A statue, giddy with desire. Adam had seen her and had understood her intentions. She felt wild and crazy and so unbelievably turned on. She was leading this seduction and he was following. She'd never done anything like this and she loved the feeling that pulsed through her veins.

And she got the impression that Adam was loving it, too.

Where had she dredged up the courage?

Her cheeks flushed hot with excitement. A mass of images filled her mind, all of them erotic and involving making full and unorthodox use of the Louvre.

Nervously Morgan studied the people filing into the room. It had been several minutes since she'd met Adam's eye in the display-case glass and winked at him.

Where was he?

Tentatively she eased from her hiding spot and crept back toward the room she'd just exited. She peeked around the corner.

Adam was lounging against a wall, his arms crossed over his chest, waiting. His eyes were half closed and he was grinning wickedly.

Dammit, he'd tricked her, making her come to him.

She darted away, heart ticking loudly in her chest, and fled this section of the museum.

This is nuts, she thought. *Everyone must know what you're up to, seducing some guy in broad daylight in a public place.*

She hurried over to stare at a painting of a dour monk praying by candlelight. She stood motionless, unseeing, her face smoldering, her body a five-alarm blaze.

Was Adam behind her? Watching?

And was there such a thing as a six-alarm blaze?

Surreptitiously she glanced over her shoulder just in time to see him disappear into a crowd of tourists heading away from her.

Ah, so Adam was leading now?

Taking a deep breath, she gulped and trailed after the group. At his height Adam was easy to spot. The group filed up a staircase. Adam turned and looked back.

Their eyes met.

His smile was more enigmatic than the Mona Lisa's. She was so busy staring at him, she tripped on the bottom step and nearly knocked into a teenage girl. Apologizing, she righted herself and looked up again, but Adam had vanished.

Excitement and anticipation built inside her. She reveled in it. More than anything she wanted him to whisk her off into some darkened corner out of sight of the security cameras. She wanted him to hold her, kiss her and run his palm up under her silk blouse. Her breast ached at the thought of being touched by his warm hands, and her insides flared with expectancy.

She reached the top of the stairs, surrounded by the echo of a thousand footsteps.

Paintings of feminine nudes lined the walls of the corridor. These women were soft and beautiful. The artist gloried in the female form. The paintings were a tribute to women's sexuality, even though they had been painted hundreds of years ago.

Had Adam lured her here on purpose, to tantalize her with these provocatively erotic paintings?

She paused to study one of the pictures. A well-rounded woman lounged on a bed beside an open window, cradling a ripe ruby-colored womb-sized pear.

Morgan could feel Adam's eyes on her, although she did not know where he was standing.

Don't look around. Don't give him the satisfaction. Pretend you've stopped playing the game.

She kept gazing at the nude, but as she stared, the colors began to kaleidoscope and she found herself caught in a memory. She could see Adam in front of her, looking as he had the first night she'd slept over at his apartment.

He'd gone into the kitchen to fix them a midnight snack and she'd trailed silently after him, watching as he'd poked around in the refrigerator. He'd been totally nude and not the least bit self-conscious. He'd bent over, his glorious backside on full display. He'd been whistling to himself, unaware that she was behind him.

His easy self-assurance was one of the things she'd admired most about him. He balanced her tendency to second-guess herself.

Hands clenched behind her back, she moved on to the next painting. This was a group of naked women sitting in a lush green field, chatting as casually as if they were clothed. Her mouth grew dry. She could tell that he was near, but she would not allow herself to look around.

Play it cool.

By nature, she might tend toward questioning herself, but she'd become a master at not letting her insecurities show.

But it was hard playing it cool when her heart was banging around in her chest like a tin can being kicked through the street. Imperceptibly she turned her head, acting as if she were studying the gradations of color in the painting.

From her peripheral vision she caught a glimpse of a man's black shoe, polished to a high sheen, positioned just behind her and a few feet to her left.

Only an image-conscious man wore that particular brand of expensive shoes. It had to be her man.

What to do now?

Had he lobbed the ball back in her court? Should she turn and flee? Or turn and confront him?

Which would be more fun?

For a full minute she stood there, unable to decide but achingly aware that he was behind her. She could smell his scent, so masculine, so Adam.

Without looking at him, she spun to her right and marched away, following the directional signs pointing to the ladies' lounge. She pushed through the door, stepped inside, closing him out.

The lounge was nicely decorated with mirrors for primping and two high-backed couches for sitting. Beyond the lounge area lay the restroom. She heard women in there laughing and gossiping.

Breathing hard, Morgan rushed into a stall and locked the door behind her. She took three deep breaths, forcing herself to calm down.

Would he follow her in here?

Adam, the man who was mortified at the mere thought of public embarrassment? Not likely.

Probably he'd just skulk around outside.

She stood there, waiting for her heart rate to slow, wondering whether she should abandon the game or come up with a new strategy. Then she heard the outer door of the lounge open.

"Excuse me," a man's voice said. It wasn't just any man's voice but Adam's deep timbre. "Excuse me, ladies, but I'm with the Louvre and we're closing down the ladies' lounge temporarily. Could you please finish your business and leave as quickly as possible."

What? Morgan slapped a hand over her mouth to keep from laughing aloud. She couldn't believe it! Adam was posing as a museum employee and running the visitors out of the bathroom. What did that wicked man have in mind?

Never in a million years would she have imagined him doing something so unexpected. Aroused beyond measure, she licked her lips and listened as the women filed out of the lounge.

Silence followed.

Was Adam still in the lounge? Pressing her ear against the door, she strained to listen.

She heard the sound of a lock being snapped closed. He was barricading the door to the lounge. Sealing them in.

Panic tinged, but monumental excitement overwhelmed her. He was being so bad and she loved it, yet at the same time she was incredibly nervous.

Trying to be as quiet as she could, she climbed up on the toilet seat and ducked her head so it wouldn't show over the top of the stall.

She heard the sound of footsteps first whispering

across the carpet in the lounge, then slapping against the tile floor of the restroom. She put a hand to her head and brushed back a lock of hair. The erotic sensations inside her built, turning to liquid fire.

This was nuts! But she felt so damned sexy. Adam had risked so much to come after her.

He was moving through the bathroom. She heard the creak of a stall door and her gut tightened.

Was he as excited as she? Was he rock-hard and ready for her? Was chasing after her driving him as wild as it was driving her?

She heard him open another stall door and then another, his steps coming closer, ever closer to where she was hiding.

Crazily her breasts filled hotly with blood, and she knew immediately when he reached the door behind which she hid. He stopped in front of it and reached out to turn the knob, but she had locked it against him.

"Mademoiselle," he said in a horrible rendition of a French accent. She smiled at his effort. "This is the museum authority. You must come out. We know you have stolen a valuable piece and hidden it somewhere on your person. Our surveillance cameras caught you, and it is my job to do a full-body search."

She did not answer. She was breathing too hard to speak.

He rattled the door. "Best make it easy on yourself, *mademoiselle,* and come out of your own free will. Don't make me take the door off its hinges."

"Perhaps—" she started but had to clear her throat "—we can make a deal."

"What kind of deal?"

"I give you back the valuable museum piece and you let me go."

"But you are a thief, *mademoiselle*. The management of the Louvre frowns very severely on having their antiques stolen by beautiful American women. You must face the music."

"What if I were to give you sexual pleasures in exchange for my freedom?" she dared.

"I am listening."

"Stand back and I'll come out."

She heard him take two steps back. Morgan got down off the toilet seat and slid the lock back. Slowly she opened the door and stepped out to find her husband staring, mesmerized, at her.

"We won't be disturbed?" she asked.

"I placed a Bathroom Being Cleaned sign outside the door."

"Where did you get it?" Her gaze held his. There was no mistaking the lust in his eyes.

"A staff member of the Louvre has his secrets. Now about those sexual pleasures you promised?"

"I am yours to do with me as you wish, as long as you do not call the *gendarmes* on me."

He seized her hand and led her back into the lounge area. Taking her by the shoulders, he positioned her in front of the mirrors while he stood behind her.

"Strip," he ordered.

Not knowing from where her daring sprang, Morgan eagerly obeyed his command. Her fingers quivered as she unbuttoned the top button of her blouse. One by one, she twisted the buttons open, exposing the pristine white lace of her bra.

An incredible heat permeated her body. When the last button was undone, she slid both the blouse and her ginger-colored jacket off her shoulders and let them drift to the ground.

It felt so wanton, so erotic to be playing this thrilling sex game. How many times had she imagined such intriguing trysts, yet believed it would never happen?

But Adam had come through for her. He'd followed her here and joined in her fantasy.

Love for him overflowed her heart. He was trying so hard to please her.

Enveloped in the musky glow of eroticism, she unzipped the side zipper of her tailored trousers. She tried to act nonchalant, slipping her pants down, but it was a ruse. Her palms were slick, and in the mirror she watched her torso flushing red with desire.

As she finished removing her clothes, Adam remained standing behind her, watching.

In the mirror she saw him unzip his pants, take his hard flesh in his hand. He looked as wild as she felt. Strange and new and crazy with wickedness.

Her breasts ached. She licked her lips. And Adam did the same.

She unhooked her bra. The skimpy material floated away from her body. Then she put one finger under the waistband of her panties. Lingeringly she tugged them down over her hips.

The sensations washing over her were gloriously naughty. And then she was completely nude and so turned on she thought she might come right then and there, watching him watching her in the mirror.

She cupped her breasts, eyeing him coyly, egging him on.

He came up behind her.

She swallowed desperately, felt his hard manhood throbbing from the folds of his pants. He pressed himself against her naked back and she felt him growing harder still. Brushing aside her hair, he lowered his head and gently kissed the nape of her neck.

The hot wetness of his lips ignited her, and the waves of passion that had been rising inside her flowed like molten lava.

"Take me," she demanded hoarsely. "Stake your claim, use me...."

With frantic movements he stripped off his pants and then lifted her up.

Instinctively she knew what he wanted and wrapped her legs around his waist. He pressed her back against the cool, smooth glass of the mirror and then pulled her down onto his demanding shaft.

She slid onto him like baby oil and, in shock, realized she was already coming. He pumped into her until

Morgan felt as if she were being split in two by his massive size. She bit down on her lip to keep from crying out as the first orgasm abated only slightly before bursting boldly into a second one.

Her entire body contracted in a series of mind-altering spasms.

Then he spun her around and positioned her in front of the mirror so she could watch, too. Wide-eyed, she stared, mesmerized by the sight as he entered her over and over again until they were blasted into a blinding blowout together.

KING OF THE JUNGLE.

Adam couldn't contain his glee. He felt like a proud male lion. He wanted to throw back his head and roar.

What a rush!

And as for his Morgan, she was unbelievable. He had no idea she could be so sensual, so uninhibited. She'd impressed him.

They were holding hands, walking back toward the La Fontaine, not speaking, basking in the afterglow of the most exciting sex they'd ever enjoyed.

"You hungry?"

"Absolutely." She looked at him, a smug, dreamy smile of satisfaction on her face. Now he understood why the Mona Lisa looked the way she did. The Louvre was chock-full with delightful secrets.

"How about this place?" Adam nodded at a little café just up ahead.

"Perfect."

He draped his arm around her shoulder and pulled her closer to him. She snuggled against his chest.

Morgan had been right. Something special had been missing from their relationship and for quite some time. She'd gone through a transformation last year and he'd watched it happen. He'd admired both her bravery and her indomitable spirit, but at the same time those alterations made her a stronger person, he'd felt as if she'd somehow grown beyond him and he had no idea how to catch up.

But now, the chemistry was back stronger than ever. If she'd come here planning on having an affair, surely what had just happened in the Louvre had changed all that. Morgan was a loyal woman. If he was giving her the attention she needed, she wouldn't throw away ten years of marriage for a fling.

One great shag in the Louvre isn't going to solve all your problems. She needs more. She deserves more. You've been taking her for granted and you know it.

It was well after the lunch hour and the café had thinned out. They were seated immediately at a cozy table near a window overlooking the street.

Adam gazed at his wife as if seeing her for the first time. The rich luster of her butternut-colored hair, the warmth in her wide brown eyes, the inquisitive tilt to her head as she regarded him intently. He was the luckiest man in the world and he'd been blinded to his good fortune until the threat of another man had alerted him to his neglect.

"Adam," she said once they'd placed their orders and were gazing deeply into each other's eyes, "I can't begin to tell you how much it means to me that you came to France."

"I had to come," he said and took a deep breath. *Go ahead and tell her how much she means to you. It's what she needs to hear.* "I was afraid that if I didn't, I would lose you forever."

Her smile disappeared and her eyes darkened. "I was afraid of that, too."

His chest tightened. "Is there something you want to tell me?"

"What do you mean?"

"Is the real reason you came to France alone to teach me a lesson or…" He swallowed, not knowing how to express the fear inside him.

"Or what?"

"Did you come to meet a lover?" he blurted, unable to stand the anxiety one second longer.

"A lover?" She stared at him as if he'd sprouted a third eye on his chin.

"I mean, I can't blame you if you did. I've taken you for granted. I realize that now."

"You think I came to France to have an affair?"

"Well, I didn't believe that until I found an instant message on your computer screen from some guy named Henri Renouf."

"You were snooping around on my computer?"

"No, not intentionally. My zip drive gummed up and

I went to use yours, and you'd left your computer on and forgotten to log off the Internet." He reached out to her. "Please, just tell me, what does this guy mean to you? Are we in serious trouble?"

She said nothing.

In the space of the pause their waiter brought them big bowls of onion soup, crusty yeast bread and cups of hot spiced tea, but neither of them noticed the food.

Adam held his breath, waiting, tortured, tormented by the dread that she was going to tell him that she was madly in love with this Renouf character and wanted a divorce.

"Are you jealous of Henri Renouf?" she asked, and damn if there wasn't a spark of amusement in her eyes.

"Hell, yes."

"Why, Adam—" she peeked at him through lowered lashes "—I can't remember the last time you were jealous over me."

"You've never given me a reason to be jealous. Until now." Adam fisted his hands.

Morgan noticed his reaction. "You'd fight for me?" She said it as if the idea excited her.

"If Renouf was here right now, I'd plow my fist through his face on general principle," he said, vehemently meaning every word.

She burst out laughing.

Adam's face flamed hot. "What? What is it? What's so funny?"

"That's why you followed me to France? You thought I came here to have an affair with Henri Renouf?"

"It's not funny, Morgan."

"Hmm," she teased. "If I'd known an affair would light a fire under you, I might have considered having one a long time ago."

"Just tell me the truth." He gritted his teeth. "It's eating me up inside. I gotta know where I stand."

Morgan's face softened with love and she reached out to lay a palm over his hand. "Sweetheart, I'm not now, nor have I ever had an affair. There's never been anyone for me but you. You know I'd never stray."

Adam felt as if all the air had been sucked from his body. She wasn't having an affair. Thank God. And he believed her. Not just because he wanted to but because his wife was the most honest person he knew. She did not lie. But just because she was not having an affair did not mean that he was off the hook. She'd shared something important with Renouf. His instant message had been inviting, flirty. The man was filling some kind of need for her that he was not and for that reason Adam was almost as jealous as he would have been over a physical affair.

"So who is this Henri Renouf?" he asked, trying to sound casual.

"He's an antiques dealer who has somehow managed to get his hands on the White Star amulet."

"The White Star," he muttered.

He knew Morgan had become passionately involved in unraveling the mystery of the ancient box, the amulet and the legend, but honestly he hadn't paid much attention to her fixation.

"Henri Renouf lives in the south of France. I came here to meet him, to see what's inside the box. To find out if it really did belong to Egmath and Batu."

"That's what's so important to you?" His shoulders sagged in relief. This was all about her curiosity with those star-crossed lovers. "It's all about the box. Nothing else?"

"Yes."

"Oh."

"Are you disappointed that you made a mad dash across the Atlantic for nothing?"

"No, no, not at all. I'm very happy to be here, especially after that sensational welcome at the Louvre." He winked. "This has been a reminder for me not to take what we have for granted."

"What about Davidson? What about the Jacobbi prospectus?" she murmured. "What about your promotion? It's important to you too and the timing is bad, coinciding with our tenth anniversary. I did put you between a rock and a hard place."

"None of that is as important as you are," Adam said, and even though he meant every word of it, there was an uneasiness tapping at the back of his brain, urging him to come clean. He should just come right out and tell her that he had to be back in New York by Monday morning. That he hadn't told Davidson he was coming to France.

But her smile was so bright and she looked so darned happy. And the fact that she was so obsessed with that box of hers and the legend of its star-crossed lovers told Adam that she desperately needed some magic in her life. Magic he hadn't been providing. He couldn't bear to disappoint her again.

So what are you going to do?

If only there was some way he could be with Morgan and work on the Jacobbi account at the same time.

There you go again, trying to stretch yourself too thin. Trying to have it all.

What was so damned wrong with trying to have it all? He wanted a great marriage and a high-powered career and a nice life. Was it too much to ask? Or were his priorities totally skewed?

The tender way his wife was looking at him jerked Adam's heart. Morgan deserved his full attention, but no matter how much he might wish things were different, he just couldn't give her his all.

Morgan squeezed his hand. "I think what happened at the Louvre is only the beginning. Wait and see."

And then he had an idea of how he could both titillate his wife and get some work done.

It was underhanded. It wasn't fair to either Morgan or Davidson, but it was the perfect solution as long as neither one of them knew what he was up to.

"I have a plan for doing exactly that," he said.

"Yes?" She leaned forward.

He took out a credit card and pushed it across the table. He told himself he wasn't buying her off, that he was feeding her fantasies. "Go shopping," he said. "Buy something sexy. Then go back to your hotel room and wait for my call."

"Where will you be?"

"Planning a night you'll never forget."

And, whispered his obnoxious conscience, *working on Jacobbi's prospectus while she's shopping and primping and anticipating.*

She tucked his credit card into her purse, her eyes aglow. "This is so amazing, Adam. I can't wait."

She beamed at him and he forced himself to smile back, while in his head he was wincing at his own chicanery. In the span of one quick lunch he had gone from feeling like the king of the jungle to feeling like a common garden slug.

9

ADAM'S DEVILISH PLAN was driving her mad with desire, and Morgan could think of nothing else but being with him again. It was as if he was the perfect stranger she had known forever, waiting for her, in the shadows, just out of reach. She'd never felt so inspired, poised on the threshold of something phenomenal.

But as her excitement built, so did her anxieties. Yes, what he'd proposed was special, intoxicating, arousing. It was a wonderful extension of what had transpired in the Louvre that afternoon and everything she'd been dreaming of. It was mysterious and alluring and novel. His romantic game was not the problem, but rather it was his motivation that gave her some small measure of concern.

She caught a glimpse of her reflection in the window glass. Cool woman, wild hair. Cultivated pearls at her throat, unruly perfume. Sophisticated black dress but with no panties on underneath.

Who was she becoming?

The phone rang. Heart pounding, Morgan picked it up.

"The Cabaret Champagne," Adam said, gave her the address and then hung up.

A seductive dance show was in progress when Morgan entered the Cabaret Champagne and thankfully most everyone's attention was focused on the performance. A cluster of bistro tables encircled the stage. At the back of the room stretched a long bar with lots of polished glass mirrors.

She saw him before he saw her.

He was sitting at the end of the bar, two full martini glasses in front of him filled with an intriguing blue liquid.

He was looking down and caught sight of her ankle as she came to stand beside him. His gaze followed the length of her leg on up her body to her face, and he inhaled an audible breath in the space between them as their eyes made contact.

The way he looked at her made her feel so intensely female. The satiny material of her dress rubbed against her bare breasts, stroking the nipples into taut peaks. He noticed and wet his lips.

At the rush of sexual awareness, she clamped her knees together, remembering she wore no underwear.

A dastardly grin transformed his face, carving sexy grooves like parentheses around his mouth. *And you just thought things were wild at the Louvre,* that grin said.

She was so excited she could scarcely breathe. She had been with him over a decade, and here she was, feeling his presence in a way she'd never quite felt it before.

What was it? An added edginess to the old tug and

tingle, casting it anew. Making her see details she'd overlooked, missed.

He was strong and taut-skinned, with biceps that bulged tightly beneath the sleek silk of his shirt. This man was hers and yet she felt as if she barely knew him. She had stroked her fingers over those muscles many times, but now she longed to touch him in as many ways possible. Not just with her tongue or her hands but with her nose, her forehead, her chin, her cheek.

There was so much about him still left to explore, and she couldn't wait to get started. As she climbed up on the stool beside him, careful to keep her legs crossed, he pushed the martini glass toward her and said simply, "Ice Blue."

The music was loud and it was difficult to hear each other.

"To seizing the moment," she said and lifted her glass for a toast.

He touched his glass to hers and their gazes held.

She raised it to her lips and took a sip. The drink tasted like a winter wonderland, like frozen bubbles. Crisp and cool and secretive but with an undercurrent of whimsy.

How accurately he had captured her mood with this choice of drink. She dragged a stuttering breath into her lungs, anxious and ready for the action to begin, eager to know exactly what he had in mind.

Two more long swallows to bolster her courage and the drink was gone.

She felt hot and reckless.

He spoke to the bartender, a round-faced young woman with hair dyed jet-black and skin as pale as bleached flour. The woman smiled at him invitingly.

Jealousy bit her.

Back off, sister. She threw the message like a dagger with her eyes. Possessively Morgan placed her hand over Adam's.

The bartender turned away.

Adam cocked his head and smiled at her. "Don't worry," he said. "I only have eyes for you."

God, he'd seen right through her.

"I'm not the least bit worried."

"You lie."

"You think?" She caught his gaze.

"I know. Besides, turnabout is fair play. You really had me sweating over Henri Renouf."

"Maybe a little jealousy is a good thing. Keeps us on our toes."

"It's wicked is what it is. I hate the thought of someone else touching you."

"You should tell me that more often and I should do the same for you."

In answer, he just growled and pushed a hand through his dark blond locks. His hair had grown out a little, she realized. It was past time when he would normally get it trimmed and it teased the edge of his collar. She liked it longer.

Morgan watched him toy with a cocktail straw,

crimping the red plastic between his index finger and thumb. He talked the silence away, telling her what the cabaret show was about.

He hadn't shaved since that morning, which wasn't like him. Adam was always neat and well-manicured, and that fact intrigued her. Had he purposely left the stubble as part of this new seduction? The dusty glaze of beard at his chin lured her, and she had to reach for her glass to keep herself from stroking it.

She licked her lips.

He winked.

They were sliding toward old patterns in their flirtation, easing into what was familiar. It was a challenge to break the habit. But they must. It was time for something new.

"What now?" she asked.

"There's viewing booths where we can watch the show in private." He nodded at the stage.

Morgan glanced around and for the first time noticed there was an upper floor to the cabaret that ringed the stage with tinted windows peering out onto the action below.

He said something to the bartender again, slipped her money, and she passed him a key. He slid off his stool, slipped into his suit jacket and then turned to settle his big warm palm against the small of her naked back. From the stage there came a distant pounding, but it sounded like the drum roll inside her own head.

The performers danced erotically, their moves simulating sex acts.

He led her down a narrow corridor. The walls were

covered in a cloth of crushed black velvet. Christmas rope lights twinkled from recesses in the ceiling.

It felt like midnight. Dark and breathless.

Her head swam with erotic possibilities. She felt delirious, as if wandering through a feverish mirage.

The cuffs and collar of his white silk shirt peeped from around his charcoal-gray jacket. In this lighting he looked like a puma ensconced in men's clothing. Good breeding and charming words could not disguise his raw magnetism. He possessed an animalistic sexuality she'd never truly been aware of before now.

How had this magnificent man become her husband?

There was a stairway at the end of the corridor. He guided her up it, one creaking wooden step at a time. When they got to the top of the landing, he draped his arm around her shoulder and drew her close to him.

Before them lay another black-velvet-lined corridor filled with doors painted starkly glossy white. But where the corridor below had been straight, this one was bent in a skinny half-moon shape.

Their breathing was ragged and out of sync. She could still taste the lingering flavor of gin from the Ice Blue drink. A tide of longing surged between them— she could feel it in his body heat.

Adam shepherded her forward around the half-moon circle, the key the bartender had given him clutched in his hand. He stopped in front of one of the white doors, and Morgan thought it was pretty prophetic that it was number ten.

The room was a small, perfectly symmetrical square and totally devoid of furnishings except for a small wooden bench positioned in front of the window that overlooked the stage below. In here the walls were also covered with rich black velvet, as well as the floors and the ceiling.

It felt as if they were standing inside a jewelry box. The only light in the room came from the white rope lights chasing along all four sides of the window, a winking synchronized pattern of illumination.

Adam kicked the door closed with his foot, then turned to twist the lock, shutting them up together in this odd space.

She was a little afraid to stray from him, the weirdness of the unfamiliar washing over her. She inhaled the masculine musk of him, which echoed with a woodsy redolence, like fresh stalks of rosemary.

His teeth flashed white in the darkness as he smiled at her, his mouth set in that familiar curl that chased away the weirdness. She smiled faintly in return but then shifted her gaze from the customary to the novel, the fresh whiteness of his new shirt as he slipped off his jacket and let it drop to the floor.

He moved closer to her, cupped his palm against the nape of her neck and lifted her head up to meet his. He brushed his lips over hers.

It was a surprisingly tender kiss that sped an electrical charge over her skin. He threaded his fingers through her hair, got tangled in her new undisciplined style.

While his hand was still caught in her hair, she skimmed her fingertips down the front of his smooth silk shirt, felt the hard, comforting ladder of muscles stretching from his chest to his abdomen.

Slowly she began undoing each button, still tight in their newness.

Speakers were mounted in all four corners of the ceiling, piping in music from the cabaret show. A throaty-voiced woman sang a mournful French song about the perils of loving too much. Morgan had heard the song on the radio several times since she'd arrived in the city and she found herself singing along in French.

The song was hypnotic, compelling. Her hips twitched in time to the sultry rhythm. She fell into the song, let it engulf her as she danced.

Adam leaned back against the door, his eyes heavy-lidded as he watched her sway. She kicked off her shoes, sank her feet into the thick, cushioned velvet, curling her toes into the soft material.

Cloud dancing.

The tempo of the music increased, and Morgan followed it, gyrating closer to her lover, almost touching him but not quite.

He cocked his hips toward her, the back of his shoulders still resting against the door.

And she began a striptease, spiraling her hips, swaying back and forth, she stepped back from him, allowing the music to swell up through the bottom of her feet to the pit of her stomach. She let it seduce her senses. She unfolded into it.

Turning her back to Adam, Morgan reached up and started inching down the zipper of her dress. She glanced over her shoulder to watch him, offering up a sly smile. He nodded his appreciation.

More.

His blue-gray eyes were so intense, so hot, the burn of it rippled across her flesh. The look on his face mirrored the mixture of barely leashed passion and liberated fantasy surging through her body.

Lower and lower she slipped the zipper. Losing her old self, shedding a skin. She felt decadent and powerful and womanly.

She slid the black silk dress from first one shoulder, then the other. For a moment she held the dress teasingly to her breasts with one hand and then she moved her arm and let it fall slowly so that it pooled at her feet and blended into the inkiness of the black velvet floor.

He groaned when he saw she was now standing nude before him. "You didn't wear any underwear," he croaked.

"No."

He swallowed hard. "That's so hot."

"I walked across town totally naked under my dress."

"Torturous wench," he murmured deep and low, his voice almost a growl.

She ran her palms over her body and wriggled as she

caressed her curves. Lowering her lashes, she blew him a kiss, the sweet smacking sound echoing in the empty confines, in the silence between the stage music.

A new song started. This one she did not know and she danced closer to him again. Breathing in sync with the throbbing beat, she flicked out her tongue and ran it along her lips, enticing him to dance.

Follow me, she commanded with her eyes and brushed her naked breasts against the smooth material of his shirt, grazed them over the bareness of his chest peeping out through the buttons she'd undone.

She writhed against him.

He reached out to touch her, but she quickly moved away. Taunting him. His hand dropped through the air as she moved backward toward the viewing window, toward the sound, toward the light.

He stalked toward her, grim determination sitting on his face. He looked like a stranger in the shadows. Not just a stranger but an alien. Foreign and mysterious. Who was this man?

He's unknowable, she thought, and fear was a sudden tumult in her heart.

The back of her knees bumped into the solid, resistant surface of the wooden bench. It felt as hard as his body cloaked beneath the civilized exterior of his clothing.

He drilled his enigmatic eyes into her. She was both scared and extremely aroused.

She rubbed herself over him. Moving up and down, around and behind. Her breasts over his chest, her back along his shoulders, her pelvis against his hip. Strands of her riotous hair caught on the whiskers at his jaw.

A heady sigh escaped her lips at the surge of scarcely harnessed tension sweltering from his tightened muscles. This time he did not try to feel her with his hands but allowed his body to intercept the sensations she was putting out.

Closing his eyes, he whispered softly, "I love the sway of your breasts against my shoulder blades. I love the way your rhythm is building inside me."

She loved it, too. She snaked against him, stretching like a cat. She bumped her bare buttocks across the seat of his pants and grinned when he groaned.

Then she spun around and danced back in front of him. He locked his eyes with hers and lightning arced between them.

His head descended, came close, so close, almost to her lips but not quite. His warm breath hovered, daring her to make the first move.

She muttered a strangled cry of frustration and gave in, grabbing hold of his tie, pulling his head all the way down.

He smashed his mouth against hers. The pungent scent of his desire rose through the erotic fragrance overlying his skin. His arms wrapped around her waist, his hands splaying over the curve of her ass, drawing her close, locking her against him.

She uttered a low ensnared sigh and pushed herself flush against his burgeoning hardness.

Adam moved with her, thrusting his hips, their bodies

fused as he took the lead, bringing her with him as he followed the music seeping from the speakers.

She lay her head against his chest, her ear pressed to his heart.

With one hand he traced the line of her spine, trailing a finger over each little ridge, kneading, touching.

Heaven. His embrace was heaven.

But it was not enough. She wanted more. Wanted him filling up her body with his long, hard erection. She separated from him, pulling away, then sinking slowly to the floor. She settled her butt onto the soft crushed velvet.

She stretched out, lounging on her hip, propping herself up on one elbow, sleek and lithesome as a tigress. The velvet puckered in ruches around her, like ocean ripples.

Adam stood over her, watching with a lustful gaze. He whipped off his shirt and tie, threw them behind him. They landed on the bench.

He was backlit in the glow from the lights chasing around the window. He shone, the vibrant halo stroking his strong lines and angles.

Coquettishly she drew one leg to her chest, exposing her inner thigh and offering him a tantalizing glimpse of her sex. She caressed a breast with one hand, gently pinched her nipple between her thumb and index finger, intentionally driving him crazy.

He wasn't accustomed to her acting so unbridled, but neither was she. It felt good. She felt unchained.

Groaning, Adam shucked off his belt, briefs and

trousers and kicked them aside, revealing the masculine key that would unlock her femininity.

He dropped to his knees beside her.

"I gotta have you, babe," he said huskily. "I can't take this torture one minute longer."

She dipped a finger into her mouth and suckled softly. She took that wet finger and ran it along her lower lip, tracing a damp path over her chin to her throat and then on down past her swollen, straining breasts to nestle against the triangle of her pubic hair.

Closing her eyes, she moaned softly, calling to him.

He clamped a gentle hand over the fleshy softness of her buttocks. The ferocious sensations that flew out from his masculine grasp were too divine. They spread like liquid mercury, rolling quicksilver over her raw nerve endings, and then sank slowly to enter the very marrow of her bones.

The tension was so horribly sweet. It flowed from him into her, seeping deep. She rolled over onto her back, let her legs drop open, dampened her finger once more and touched herself again.

He watched, eyes sparking with the excitement of newness, of adventure, of the unexpected.

Encouraged by his approval, she sank her finger into the folds of her sex, slicking against the moisture inside of her. As her finger inched deeper to explore her wetness, she saw his body tense, seething in response.

His full-on erection jutted upright. The music whispering through the room called to some intrinsic force within them while their lips joined in a frenzy of urgency and stark, hot need.

She sank her fingertips into his shoulders. The scent of her sex was heavy in the room. His teeth nipped at her bottom lip, biting spicily but not hard.

He whispered softly against her throat.

She threaded her fingers through his hair, tugged tenderly.

He nibbled her earlobe.

She pinched one of his nipples.

He outlined her collarbone with his tongue, his penis pressing hard against her belly.

She reached down and took him in her hand, her breath passing slow and erratic over her swollen lips. Gently she massaged the potent, vital head of him, enjoying the feel of his smooth, hot ridge. With adoring, familiar strokes, she fondled him, working him to a fevered pitch before guiding him to the heat that awaited inside her.

He gave a strangled cry and sank inside of her. His voice tore as he whispered, "You make me whole."

As he rode her body to the core, she felt something wonderful expanding in her chest. This is what she'd been looking for. This heady, crazy lustiness that spoke of so much more than mere sex.

The hard shaft of his naked flesh bowed inside her. Their skin tingled, their scents joined, the mysterious undercurrent of their animal origins entwining together. Her legs slid around him. She pulled him in deeper.

When the tip of him pressed against the spot that had ached for the pressure of his penis, she closed her eyes over the sensation, wanting to hold on to it. She tightened the muscles of her sex around him in a ferocious embrace as she arched her hips upward.

"Slow down, you minx," he said. "Don't make me come this soon."

Her breath caught. Realizing he was right and that she wasn't ready for the fun to end, Morgan tried to force her body to relax. But she wanted him so damned badly she couldn't stop squeezing him.

"Hey, hey." He grabbed her wrists and gently pinned her to the floor.

Panting, he slowly pulled out of her, the head of him throbbing hard against her straining cleft.

She fought him for escape, her back arching upward, her wrists twisting beneath the hands that held her prisoner, making her wilder, more desperate for him. She wanted nothing more than to grab his beautiful ass and haul him back down inside of her until he made her come. She was insane with the desire. Out of control.

"Easy, easy, sweetheart," he whispered. "Just give me a minute."

"Take me," she begged. "I have to have you. Please, please."

The cry was ripped from her throat as he plunged into her again, giving her exactly what she begged for. She gasped, elated to have him back again.

Like caged beasts they went at it, starving for release. They roared inside their captive space, rolling over and over across the room, tumbling like wrestlers on top of the padded velvet carpet. First her on top, then him. Flipping without ever separating, the two of them fused by an age-old passion, until he was back on top again. King of the jungle.

Her hips forged up against his, meeting him thrust for thrust, her grappling hands clutching at his shoulders. The release of pent-up energy shot through her sensation after sensation.

They rode fast and hard, but there was no outrunning the blaze. It closed in on them with each masterful stroke. It beat against them relentlessly. He roared, a beast unleashed, and she was right with him, her legs locked tightly around his waist.

Limbs arched, she bowed up beneath him, manipulating her pelvis against his. She wanted them to come together, in a simultaneous crescendo.

The fire thrust undulating waves of heat through the flesh of her sex. She was cinched in the grip of passion, her body eagerly absorbing what she needed from him.

As the feeling of weight descended upon her womb and the final spasms rippled through her at the same time she felt them rip through him, she drew his body close against her, holding him lovingly in her arms.

He clung to her, his body cradled against hers, their limbs entwined. Morgan kissed his face sweetly, lightly. Her lover. Her husband.

"Thank you for this," she whispered. "Thank you."

Tonight they'd taken a big step toward bridging the gap between them, and for the first time in months Morgan felt truly hopeful about their future.

10

THE FOLLOWING MORNING Adam took Morgan to a lavish Sunday brunch at the La Fontaine. Afterward, he proposed a visit to the top of the Eiffel Tower.

"Isn't this romantic?" She breathed in the city as they strolled the streets, arm in arm. "Time alone for the two of us. No work, no cell phones, no e-mail. Just you and me and Paris."

This was the right time, she thought, and the place. To say all the things she hadn't been able to say to him at home. To try her very best to close the gap between them. They'd made a wonderful start. She would build on that fragile bridge.

"Not just romantic," he said huskily, draping his arm around her shoulder and pulling her closer to him, "but sexy as hell. I still can't believe the way you were last night at the Cabaret Champagne. You shocked and surprised me. I especially enjoyed the striptease. I've never seen you so inhibited and this new side of you turns me on like crazy."

Adam gazed at her and Morgan's chest tightened. A strand of hair had fallen softly across his forehead and his eyes were aglow. He smelled of autumn, like pumpkins and nutmeg and cool morning mist.

"I'm finding out that I have many facets of my personality I was too busy to explore before." She fingered a button on his coat. "I'm betting you have unknown facets too."

"Morgan…" he started to say something else, but he stopped.

"Yes?" She looked into his eyes again and she was curious to see remorse written on his face.

"We have been missing out on a lot."

Yes, oh, yes. This was the realization she'd been hoping he would reach. "It's okay," she said and reached up a finger to trace his mouth. "We can fix it. Now that we've acknowledged that we got derailed, we can get our marriage back on track."

He kissed her. Right there on the street. And it was hot and rich and nurturing.

The crisp weather, their closeness, the sights and sounds of Paris crystallized into the prefect moment. She wanted to catch time in a snow globe and put it on display in their bedroom so they could shake it up whenever they were tempted to forget how truly great they were together.

He broke the kiss, took her by the hand and led her to their destination.

"How is it that we didn't go up in the Eiffel Tower when we were here the first time?" Adam asked as they joined the crowd queueing up to ride the elevator to the top of the monument.

"Um, I believe that would be because we never got out of bed."

"Oh, yeah." He grinned.

They arrived at the top of the Eiffel Tower and Morgan rushed to the railing to peer over, giddy with excitement. "Come look, Adam and see how far you can see."

She turned to glance back at him over her shoulder and the physical reality of him was a direct hit to her heart.

He was so handsome. How had she ever landed such a good-looking man?

Faded denim jeans hugged his narrow hips and a black leather jacket clung to his broad shoulders. He looked both rebellious and arty. That leather jacket gave him the aura of a bad boy with a sensitive soul. She'd never thought of him that way before. To her, he'd always been Mr. All-American—blond, clean-cut, dependable. But now he looked dangerous and wild.

A thrill chased through her. This was what she'd been longing for. A hint of the unfamiliar, a whisper of the unknown inside the man she knew so well.

As he watched her watching him, his eyes darkened with desire. They stared into each other in a way they hadn't looked in a long time.

His smile was tentative, nervous even.

In that moment she understood something about him that she'd never understood before. He worked so hard because he feared that it was the only thing of value he had to offer her. The realization sent her mind reeling.

How could she have not figured that out about him? It wasn't as he'd told her; that his work defined who he was, but rather Adam believed he had no real value as a person if he wasn't being productive. That's why he couldn't slow down. That's why he worked so hard.

She recognized this truth and her heart ached for his vulnerability, even though she didn't fully understand it. How did she go about proving to him that she loved him just as he was? That there was nothing he had to do in order to keep her?

She took his hand and drew him to the railing beside her. Paris stretched out below them, a city of glamour and bustling life. "Take it all in Adam, be in the moment. Be here with me. Forget everything else."

And then Morgan began murmuring in French.

"What are you saying?" He lifted an eyebrow in surprise.

"I'm pointing out landmarks. There's Notre Dame Cathedral and the Arc de Triomphe and the Champs Élysées."

"But you're speaking French."

"Surprise. I've been listening to foreign language tapes. I did it to impress you."

"I'm impressed. How do you say I love you in French?" He wrapped an arm around her waist.

"Je t'aime."

"Je t'aime," he repeated, looking her in the eyes. "Now say something sexy."

Blushing, she told him exactly what she wanted to do to him in French.

"I don't know what you said, but I like the sound of it." He nuzzled her neck.

She translated, whispering the explicit details in his ear.

"Wow, woman, you've changed. The Morgan I know would never say those kinds of things."

"That's what I've been trying to tell you, Adam. I'm not the Morgan I've always been. This past year has really changed me and for the better I believe, but the changes I've gone through are at the center of the problems you and I have been having."

"What do you mean?"

"I don't want the same things out of life that I used to want, Adam. The things that you still want. I feel that until we resolve the differences in our values we're going to stay at a stalemate."

"You've got my attention," he said. "I'm listening."

"In the beginning, we had a plan. We were going to throw ourselves into our work until we had enough money to buy a home and start a family and then we were going to shift our priorities to raising children."

"You don't want kids anymore?" He sounded alarmed.

"Yes, yes, I do. Very much. But the way we were headed wasn't going to leave us much time for children. Which is probably why we don't already have them. I didn't want strangers raising my kids and that's what would have happened if I'd kept my job."

"I know. I thought that was basically the reason you decided to buy the antique shop."

"That was part of it, yes. But the real reason is that I

realized how out of balance we had become. I want you to be part of our children's lives too. These eighty hour work weeks aren't going to cut it, Adam. It's not enough for me anymore."

He took her by the shoulders. "Just be patient a little while longer, sweetheart. Once I make VP things will be different."

"Yes," she muttered. "You'll be working ninety hours a week."

"You want me to quit my job, Morgan? Is that what you want?" She could hear the frustration in his voice. She was just as frustrated as he was. She wanted him to have the job he loved, but she desperately needed more from their relationship.

"I didn't marry you for what you could provide for me. I don't have to have the biggest house or the nicest car or the most expensive clothing. I married you because I love you. But it hurts my heart because it seems like you don't want to spend any time with me." Morgan took a deep breath, bolstering the courage to ask him the question she'd wanted to ask for a very long time but had been too afraid to bring herself to do it. "Why *did* you marry me, Adam?"

"What?" She could tell by the way his eyes widened that her question had caught him off guard.

"Was it because I fit in with your plans for your future? Was it just because at one time we shared the same goals and values and beliefs? Or was it because I was easy to be with and our relationship was comfortable?"

"I married you because I love you, Morgan."

"Do you? Do you really?"

"Yes!"

"Then why do you sublimate work for emotional intimacy? Have I disappointed you in some big way? Am I not sexy enough? Why don't I inspire a grand passion in you, Adam?"

He stared at her, mouth open, looking stunned. He shook his head. "Do you honestly believe that?"

Tears pushed at the back of her eyelids, surprising her. She bit down on her bottom lip and nodded.

"I don't understand." He sounded incredulous. "It's always been so easy between us."

"Exactly," Morgan said. "That's the problem. I want things to be better. I want our marriage to ripen and improve, not grow stale with age. I want us to be together because we want to be together, not because it's easy or because it's expected. I want excitement and adventure. I want romance and passion. I don't want you to be with me simply because you're not the kind of guy who reneges on his responsibilities."

She was trembling when she finished speaking; waiting anxiously to hear what he had to say.

"I can't believe you've been keeping all that inside all this time," he said ruefully. "And I can't believe I've been so oblivious to your suffering."

"Adam, it's not like that. I'm not miserable. I just know how wonderful it really could be if we both put our relationship first."

His eyes were misty and his mouth twitched. "Come here," he said and held out his arms. She melted into him. Her knees were so wobbly with emotions she was glad for the strong iron railing at her back.

Adam pressed his mouth against her ear and she realized he was trembling too. "I love you more than life itself, Morgan and I'm going to do my best to show you exactly how committed I am to making this a superior marriage."

LATER THAT AFTERNOON they arrived at the B and B in the Loire Valley. They'd rented a car so they could experience the French countryside and the two hour drive had been more fun than Adam had had in a very long time. They'd played French songs on the radio with Morgan singing sweetly in French. They'd reminisced about their early days together and the memories evoked those old falling-in-love feelings he'd almost forgotten.

He'd called Davidson before they'd left Paris and talked him into letting him work from home on Monday, but he knew he couldn't stall much longer. Eventually he would have to tell Morgan that he had to cut their trip short and return back home. But after her impassioned speech atop the Eiffel Tower and his promise to commit himself fully to their relationship, he had to find the right moment to break the news.

But in the meantime they had a full day and a half to enjoy themselves and he intended to make it the most memorable time of their lives. They were already off to a great start.

The romantic B and B was just made for rekindling romance. Morgan had chosen well. It was a converted two hundred year old farmhouse with ten cozy guest cottages nestled along the Loire River. The furnishings were quaint. Their hosts were Monsieur and Madame Renault, a charming couple in their mid-forties who smiled often and regaled them with stories of the local color as they checked in and offered many suggestions for how to spend their time in the Loire Valley.

After getting situated in their rooms, Adam suggested a scooter ride and picnic lunch by the river and Morgan eagerly agreed.

They called ahead for their picnic basket from the B and B's kitchen, and then went to rent the scooter at a local bike shop.

"Hold on to me," Adam instructed after they'd donned helmets and straddled the Vespa.

He didn't have to tell her that. She latched her arms around his strong, muscular waist and clung on for dear life. She'd never ridden a scooter before and she was a little nervous. She could do this. No problem. Right?

"Got a solid grip?"

"Uh-huh."

He started the engine and they took off down the road with a sudden spurt of acceleration. The darn thing had more get-up-and-go than she anticipated. Morgan squealed at the sensation and buried her face against his shoulder blade.

She could feel Adam chuckling, his ribs rising and falling in time with his laughter. Morgan couldn't help grinning in response. This was fun. A little scary maybe, but fun.

She breathed in the moment, swallowed it into her heart and held it close, treasuring it, savoring for the days and months and years ahead when she forgot how truly wonderful long-term love could be.

They motored through the village and around the town square filled with quaint shops. They zipped along the countryside, past vineyards and fields thick with sunflowers. She felt like they were cruising a Van Gogh masterpiece.

After several miles, Adam stopped the scooter on a river bridge. He turned to look at her over his shoulder, his slow sexy smile made her skin sizzle. He pointed to a sunflower field along the banks of the river. "Does that suit you as a picnic spot?"

"Perfect," she approved.

He guided the scooter off the bridge, bumping down the grassy embankment. Morgan squealed again and squeezed her eyes tightly shut so she wouldn't have to watch them hurtling toward the water. If he lost control…

"I'm not losing control of the bike," he said, reading the apprehensive tightening of her hands around his torso.

"Hey," she replied tartly. "You're a desk jockey, not a Hell's Angel. I'm allowed to have my doubts."

His laugh was huge and broad and seemed to encompass the air. He pulled the scooter to a stop beside the lazy azure river, killed the engine and helped her off.

"Safe and sound, my lady."

"Thank you." Morgan unfolded the blanket that came with the basket lunch, making a nest in the field of sunflowers. Adam flopped down on the blanket, kicking off his shoes and stretching out, hands cradled under his head as he gazed up at the sky.

She knelt beside him. "I haven't seen you looking this relaxed in a long time."

"France agrees with me."

"I knew it would."

"What's for lunch?" He sat up and poked nosily inside the basket.

It was chock full of goodies, including a bottle of locally grown red wine and a corkscrew; bread and cheese and olives; sausages and cold asparagus tips sautéed in balsamic vinegar and crisp fresh slices of pears. They fed each other, slipping morsels of food between open lips with eager fingers.

She probably shouldn't have kissed him in the field of vibrant sunflowers. The bright yellow smell of them mingling with the aroma of the earthy meal they'd just finished.

He was like a sunflower, her husband. Bold and showy and resilient and she couldn't resist him, had never been able to resist him.

Adam Shaw was her downfall.

She stared at the flowers rippling around them and suddenly they were inside of her, part of her and she wasn't really Morgan anymore. She still looked like Morgan but she felt like a sunflower. And she knew that Adam was loving the way her sunflower self was brushing against him with a feather light touch. She saw in his eyes that a kiss would not be enough. He was going to take her in this sea of sunflowers with the daylight glinting off her hair.

She studied his face.

He looked at her as if he'd just tumbled out of bed, his hair wild and whorled, his eyes heavy-lidded and filled with the vestiges of a fantastic wet dream. She admired his body, dressed casually in a T-shirt and cargo style khaki walking shorts. He looked solid, substantial, an athlete's body with muscular legs and a strong back.

And when he turned his head to inhale the sunflower scented breeze she saw the flex of muscle underneath his shirt move in one long ripple.

Her hands tingled, yearning to touch him. Between her legs, she ached for him. The scent of fertile rich summer soil was strong and loamy and feminine, the smell of it kicked her arousal up a notch.

Adam's eyes held hers and she knew he smelled it too, their lust, brewing. She tasted him before their lips touched completely.

He reached out and took her hand and pulled her close, running his fingers along the curve of her back.

Taking her with him, he sank down into the cushion of sunflowers, the sensation at once both scratchy and soft.

He lay on his back and she lay stretched out on top of him, staring down into his eyes, her thighs on either side of his waist. She kissed him. It suddenly felt so necessary, and discovered that he tasted like the wine-flavored pears they'd eaten.

His kiss was cautious, tentative. Not at all like his usual self-confident kiss. Weighted it seemed, with insecurity. As though he feared she was a mirage who would disappear if he kissed her too firmly.

The breeze gusted and the sunflowers rustled, blowing a wave of fluttering caresses over their skin. She touched her forehead to his, kept looking deep into his eyes and experienced her pulse shift from a saunter to a trot.

She saw the blue vein at his temple throbbing. The tempo of its beat matched perfectly the throbbing in her sex and there was all this nature between them. Earth and sky and wind and sunflowers.

More sunflowers than the brain could absorb.

In that hovering moment of time, everything changed.

He kissed her again, deeper, more heatedly. He groaned heavily and she felt the rumble of it flowing from his chest into hers and the almost painful tightening of his hands around her waist.

She wanted him desperately.

Now. She had to get his clothes off of him. Right this minute. She snatched at his T-shirt and he helped her wrestle it over his head. His skin was hot, his chest mottling red with desire.

He grabbed the front of her blouse and jerked it open. Buttons popped off, flying out into the field as loose and free as sunflower seeds.

Nimbly, he ran his hands up under her bra, pushing it aside, getting the material out of the way so he could touch her bare breasts.

Goose bumps spread over her skin, engulfing her in shivers. She was exposed, astride him in a field in broad daylight. It was a sweet, decadent sensation. Straddling his waist like she was, Morgan could feel exactly how hard he was for her.

"You are so beautiful," he said huskily. "The way the sun glints off your golden hair takes my breath away."

She closed her eyes, but she could still see the sea of sunflowers waving joyfully all around them. She was enmeshed. He was pinching her nipples, gently but firmly, sending little rockets of pleasure flying across her nerve endings.

He sat up with her legs still positioned on either side of him and laved his tongue over one of her nipples while his hand stole down and slipped between her legs to rub against the stiff denim of her jeans.

Arching her spine, she rocked back a little on the axis of his pelvis, giving him freer access. He reached for her zipper. She could hear the whisper of metal teeth as they separated.

His hand slid down the front of her pants, past the

thin wisp of g-string lace. His fingertips found her clit and she gasped at the heat of his touch.

And then he just started rocking against her, rhythmic and pleasing.

Her legs shook and she could feel the pressure of his body underneath her buttocks, pressing stiff against her. He was breathing hard and she was breathing harder and she didn't think she could bear one more minute of this torture.

In the distance they heard the sound of a tractor rev up and Morgan startled.

They were going to get caught!

She tried to break away, to pull her blouse closed around her nakedness but Adam wrapped one hand tight around her waist while pushing a finger deep inside of her.

Sucking in her breath, she let out a cry of happy surprise as a hot wave passed over her. *What bliss.*

He sat all the way up, pushing her down, her back crushing into the seep of sunflowers. Her nose filled anew with the fertile smell of them. Adam smiled down at her, his eyes mischievous. She could hear the tractor chugging, chugging, chugging.

"It's a long way off," he said.

She felt embarrassed, mortified by the thought of getting caught. But that was the old Morgan. She was different now. She could take a walk on the not-so-tame side and still maintain her dignity. She could let go, act a little smutty with her husband and still retain his respect. She'd learned that at the Cabaret Champagne.

His eyes twinkled.

Her heart clutched and in that moment she felt more in love with him than she'd ever felt before.

And the memories of France, of their honeymoon, that had escaped her until now came flooding back, dotting her brain like the English tea roses on the wallpaper in her antique shop—softly hued and whispering to her not to forget.

She remembered how proud she'd been to be with him. How lucky and precious he'd made her feel. Somehow those magical feelings had gotten buried in the mundane chores of day to day life, but they'd been there. Were still there, just waiting to be reignited. And all they had to do was notice each other again.

Awareness. That's what had been missing. They'd stopped being aware of each other in new and fresh ways. They'd stopped playing. Stopped telling each other their secret fears and wants and desires. She vowed never to let that happen again.

The shape of Adam's mouth, so provocative and kissable, unearthed other memories, other feelings. She remembered the first time he'd kissed her, how she had held her breath waiting, mesmerized by the shape of that mouth.

The sound of the tractor churned closer, escalating her excitement. She moved, shifting away from him and went for his zipper, wanting her husband's cock more than she'd ever wanted anything in her life.

Soon they were both naked, relishing in the glory of each other's bodies in the beautiful Loire Valley, far away from the old cares and concerns, far away from Adam and Morgan. Instead, they were new to each other. Starting over fresh and green. Like teenagers. New lovers, excited, giggling and exploring.

They looked into each other's eyes and smiled, embarrassed suddenly but in a good way. She reached a hand toward his face. His eyes were the most incredible color of summer, but then he closed them. He let her caress his face, his mouth, his chest, his throbbing penis but he did not open his eyes. Did not look at her again.

Was he nervous?

"Do you remember," he said. "The time we made love on that deserted beach in Maine? Before we were married."

No, he wasn't nervous. He'd been remembering.

And then they were new lovers no more, but a married couple who'd weathered many things together. Many joys and many sorrows. Ups and downs and ins and outs.

"I remember," she murmured.

"You wore the cutest little pink bikini."

"You remember what I wore?"

"Babe, there's no way I could forget that bikini. It was the first time I'd ever seen you in one and it was all I could do to keep my tongue in my mouth. The memory of it is permanently tattooed against the back of my eyelids."

"It was freezing cold, even in the middle of August."

"It was Maine."

"You said the same thing then."

"You've certainly surprised me, Morgan Elaine

Richards Shaw. I think of the girl you were back then and then I look at the woman you've become and all I can say is 'wow'. You've changed so much."

"In a good way?" She frowned.

"In a perfect way. You were so skittish in those days. Prim and proper and so afraid to rock the boat. Frolicking naked in the surf was the most daring thing we'd ever done sexually."

"Until this trip."

He opened his eyes half-way as if feeling her grin and sent her the most sinful look. She shivered in response. That look spoke volumes. *I want you,* it shouted. *As much as ever.*

"Hold on to your hat, woman, we're just getting started." He ran a lazy finger over one of her nipples which instantly hardened to a tight bud under his touch.

"Remember how you lured me to the beach?" she said.

"It took me an hour to set it up while you were taking a nap."

"You left a trail of seashells piled up along the seawall. Sand dollars, pink turbans and perfect miniature abalone spelling out *I love Morgan Richards* and an arrow pointing toward the shore. That was all it took. I tore down the path to the beach."

"The wind was whipping and your hair was all in your face," he said. "You'd never looked more beautiful to me. Mussed and magical. Like a mermaid."

"The beach was deserted and you were standing waist deep in the water because you were naked."

"I was praying that you would come along before someone else did."

"The water was so blue that day. The sand was so soft."

"In another ten years we'll say 'remember that time we made love in the sunflower field in the Loire Valley'?"

"Are you sure that you want to spend another ten years with me?"

"Now that's a very silly question," he said and covered her mouth with his, shutting out all her internal doubts.

They made love again. Slippery mouths, sweaty bodies, building up speed. Adam was the engine that could, chugging her up with him, gathering momentum. Sparks of passion flew from him as his iron-hard shaft beat against her greedy clitoris.

Pulling his mouth free from hers, he flung his head back, groaning and let out a cry of raw animal pleasure. The power of his climax took her so completely that Morgan's immediately followed dissolving what was left of her concerns. He was her man. Always had been, always would be.

Seconds might have passed or hours might have slipped by. She could not say which but at last, her eyes fluttered open and she looked up into Adam's face and her heart melted.

"I want you to know that I hear you sweetheart," he said. "I hear you and I'm doing my best to please you. I want ten more years and ten more after than and ten more after that. This is a real marriage. No half measures. Now and forever."

She tried to swallow back the tears but they over-flowed her eyelids, battered against her throat, slipped down her cheeks in rivers of joy.

"Shhh," he whispered. "It's okay. I'm here. I'm with you."

And she did cry. All the emotion she thought she had to keep dammed up flowed out of her. All those months of doubts and confusion and loneliness and missing him being there—really being there for her—came tumbling out.

She cried, her vision blurred, from tears and sunflowers and so much love.

After several minutes, Adam kissed her tears away. His breath warm against her skin. It was a tender kiss. Nothing hot or sexual about it. A kiss of contrition. Of reformation.

She held out her arms to him and he enfolded her into his embrace and hugged her tighter than he had ever hugged her before.

11

Morgan's suitcase was in their room when they got back to the B and B.

"Adam, look. The airline came through for me," she exclaimed and immediately pitched the suitcase onto the bed.

Frantically she unzipped it, tossing out piles of sweaters, and then yanked out the antique box that had held her mesmerized for months. She cradled the box to her chest.

"It's here. It's safe." She breathed an audible sigh of relief.

Watching her, Adam realized he'd had no idea exactly how much the silly box meant to her or why.

"I've got to call Henri," she said. "I have to let him know the box arrived. I can't wait to meet him. I can't wait to find out what's inside the box."

And as she talked, her face came alive. Her eyes glowed and her lips softened and her body practically vibrated with excitement.

Maybe if he could understand why she was so caught

up with the box, he could understand her longing and satisfy it. He eased down on the bed.

"Tell me about the lovers, Morgan. I know you've told me before, but I have to be honest, I didn't pay much attention. I didn't understand what it meant to you. I'm ready to listen. I want to know why Egmath and Batu are so important to you."

She beamed at him. He liked the way he felt when she looked at him that way.

"Yes, sure. I'd like that very much." She held up one finger. "Just let me call Henri Renouf first and get our meeting scheduled."

She went to the phone on the nightstand and placed the call.

Adam sat studying her. She tucked a strand of hair behind one ear as she spoke, quick and low. She moved her head, showing him her profile, and her looks changed. She had so many layers to her face. She could appear young and girlish one minute, but then with a slanting of her chin, a flash of her eyes, her smile would turn knowing and wise and she would change into an elegant, sophisticated woman. He never tired of looking at her. He didn't even hear her side of the conversation. His eyes were too full of her to listen.

She hung up the phone, turned back to him. "It's settled," she said. "Tomorrow morning we're driving to Henri's villa on the Mediterranean Sea. It's a day's journey by car. He was pressuring me to take the train, but I thought we could make a road trip of it, especially since we already have the rental car. Spend the night. Have a real adventure."

"You want to draw out the suspense." He grinned. "After all this time of dying to know what's inside the box, you're reluctant to have the thrill of it over with too soon. You love dragging things out."

Her face flushed. "You know me too well."

"We've spent enough holidays together. How many times over the past ten years did I get to celebrate my family's tradition of opening gifts on Christmas Eve?"

She grinned sheepishly. "Just once. Our first Christmas."

"Right, and you were so disappointed the next morning that all the gifts had been opened the night before that you convinced me to wait until Christmas morning from then on out. Waiting heightens the anticipation. Or so you claimed."

"And the payoff." She licked her lips, and he knew they weren't talking about Christmas morning anymore but something much more provocative.

"So let's build the tension together. Start from the beginning. Tell me the story of Egmath and Batu."

She curled up beside him on the bed and began to talk, spinning a delightful web of love and honor, duty and intrigue. She told of how Batu and Egmath had loved each from the time they were very young but how their love never came to pass.

She whispered with wistful sadness as she spoke of

how Egmath was forced to do what honor and tradition expected of him by marrying Batu's older sister. Adam listened with all his heart, drawing her into his arms, listening, really listening, to what Morgan was telling him.

Ever since they were adolescents Egmath and Batu had met secretly every evening at midnight near a grove of cypress trees. Under the stars they shared their dreams and ambitions, their lives and the purity of their love. They had been intimately emotionally entwined.

Not long after Egmath did his duty and married Anan, he was called to fight in a faraway land. An epic battle took place and Egmath was killed. The amulet Batu had given him was lost. And now it had been found again and it was the key to Morgan's box.

The fable had touched his wife deeply for a reason and Adam was determined to discover what that reason was. He heard the longing in her voice when she talked about Batu. Felt her hold her breath to keep from crying at the sadness of it. How the lovers only had that one special night where they'd made love and then it was lost to them forever.

With each hesitation, each break in her voice, he came closer to understanding her than he ever had. And as he did, he learned what she really needed from him.

For the first time Adam fully realized the significance of the box and the legend in her life. Egmath and Batu had become a symbol to her.

A symbol of deep passion, of unfulfilled longing, of lost love.

Here were clues to why his wife was asking more of him than he'd been giving her. For so many years, partly as an effort to first please her parents and then later to please him, she'd played a certain role. But when she'd dared to follow her dream and open her own shop, she'd started figuring out she was a much more complex person than she'd let the world see. What had previously been a satisfying life to her suddenly seemed too ordinary.

She feared, he suddenly recognized, that he did not love her with the kind of devotion that Egmath had loved Batu. She was worried that she did not inspire that kind of passion. She was, in effect, grieving for the magic she thought she'd missed out on.

His and Morgan's courtship had been an average one. Steady. Quiet. She had made no big demands of him nor he of her. On the face of things it had been an ideal match. But in the long haul he could see how she might look back on their romance and feel as if she'd been cheated out of a grand passion.

Outwardly neither of them was overly emotional. But underneath, Morgan teemed with intensity, and her feelings had been building and building and she had somehow forced her emotions into that wooden box she'd found. And when it was opened, Adam had no idea what would spring out.

But now he fully understood what she needed. She

needed passion. She needed magic. She needed to feel love and feel it deeply.

And Adam swore to himself that he would do everything in his power to give it to her.

"I HAVE AN IDEA," ADAM murmured, leaning in close to brush his mouth along the sweet spot at her jawline just below her ear.

"Yes?" She quivered.

"I'd like to try a role-playing game."

"Role-playing?"

"Let's pretend," he said. "Let's pretend you are Batu and I am Egmath. On that fateful first and last night they make love together."

"That sounds so hot."

"We're tragic soul mates soon to have our love forever torn asunder," he said. Her rapid breathing tipped him off to just exactly how much this scenario was turning her on.

She arched into him and he felt her nipples tighten beneath the soft material of her blouse.

But he eased her from his arms and sat her off to one side. Letting the anticipation build, the way she desired.

He walked to throw open the double doors that led out onto the wide stone balcony bathed in moonlight. Turning back toward her, he held out his hand.

"Batu," he whispered. "Come to me, my beloved."

"But I can no longer be your beloved, Egmath. You are to marry my sister on the morrow."

"But tonight is tonight." His eyes met hers, and in that

moment he felt the poignant yearning of those long-ago lovers. "And tomorrow is tomorrow."

She caught her breath in an audible sigh. "What are you suggesting, Egmath?"

He reached out a hand to cup her cheek. "I think you know, Batu."

"It would be so wrong."

"Is it so wrong?" Adam asked. He was surprised at the ease with which he'd slipped into the role of Egmath, a man torn between duty and love, "to want to be with the woman I love more than life itself?"

"But you cannot be with me. It has been decided. You must do what is right. For the good of our kingdom."

"But how can loving you be wrong?"

"Because it isn't meant to be. Anan is my sister and I do not wish to hurt her."

"Anan understands this arranged marriage is just duty."

She shook her head. "No one must find out. I won't betray her."

"We already have betrayed her, Batu. By meeting at this secret place every night. By sharing our secrets, our love and desires. Please grant us one night of physical passion to sustain us through all the lonely, empty years ahead." The words came to his lips so easily. It was almost as if Egmath's spirit was inside him, directing him, telling him what to say and do.

If he were a fanciful man, Adam might even believe he was channeling a ghost. He could literally feel the man's loneliness deep inside his soul. In a strange way he understood Egmath's dilemma, although what tormented Adam wasn't another woman but his loyalty to his job. Duty was one thing, but love was another.

"Come to me." He kept his hand outstretched, waiting.

She did not move.

Suddenly he was consumed with the fear that she would not take his hand.

"Batu…" he cooed, soft and low. "I love you, Batu."

"What's the point of being together for one night?" she cried. "Why torture ourselves?"

"Because we will be tortured either way, but if we make love, at least for one glorious night we will wholly and completely belong only to each other. Nothing can ever take that away."

Their eyes met, and in that moment they truly were Egmath and Batu.

Slowly she reached out.

He curled his fingers around hers as she took his hand and he exhaled audibly. It was as if love jettisoned through the ages, skipping throughout three thousand years. Through dreams of storied lands. Love swooped upon them, a mystic melding of sacred hearts.

Walking backward, he drew her out onto the balcony with him.

"Look," she said, gazing out at the valley below their balcony. "See how the moonlight dances through the cypress trees? Isn't it beautiful?"

"It's not the cypress trees I find so beautiful. Nothing

gives me as much pleasure as seeing your face awash in moon glow."

Shyly she reached up to touch her cheek with three fingers, her little finger curling under her chin, her thumb resting along her jaw.

He gazed at her, at the way her blond hair framed that treasured face. He leaned close to comb his finger through the fine, soft strands. He stroked from her scalp to the curling ends. Over and over until his fingers became entangled in the pale drapery of hair. It made him think of polished gold, with a gloss so opulent that the mere sight of it tumbling about her shoulders hardened him.

Adam felt more virile than he'd ever felt. He was lucky. That one night of impotency had been a fluke. Thank God.

And the way she was looking at him only served to ignite his passion.

He pulled her flush against his chest. Latched his mouth to hers and kissed her hard. Her pulse was racing. He felt it thundering under his lips.

Her lavender scent wafted around him, as intoxicating as the nectar of her lips.

Nothing had prepared him for what their role-playing fantasy of Egmath and Batu was doing to him. It filled him with both love and longing. They deserve magic. They had allowed the mundane ins and outs of daily life to creep in and diminish their marriage. Adam would never make that mistake again.

Because he loved his wife.

He loved her crooked little smile and her determined chin. He loved her resolve and her courage. He loved the way her eyes lit up when she spied him unexpectedly in a crowd.

He'd had all his heart ever desired and he'd taken it for granted.

Never again.

With his tongue he traced the pale blue vein that ran along her jaw to the hollow of her throat. She surrendered herself to him and he slowly began to undress her.

Her blouse slid down her body, the satiny material pooling at her feet. Then he unsnapped her jeans and eased them over her thighs. She stepped from the circle of material, kicked it aside and stood before him in nothing but a modest white cotton bra and matching white cotton panties.

He heard the sound of his own heartbeat slamming inside his head, heard himself gasp. He leaned forward and kissed the bare warm pink flesh of her upper chest.

Viewing her barely clad body, his mind registered a series of random images. Taut flat stomach, small perky breasts, a peek of nipple pushing though the lace of her bra.

Ten years, and in his eyes she was more beautiful than the day he had met her.

Slipping down, he gave his attention to her breasts. He unhooked her bra, eased the strap over her shoulders before teasing her nipples with his tongue, flicking them until they responded.

Softly she moaned and arched her back and clung to him, breathing in short, hot rasps as she rubbed herself against him.

He was hard for her. So damn hard.

He forgot they were playing Egmath and Batu. The years fell away and they were young college students again, making out in her dorm room, knowing her roommate could walk in at any minute. Hormones rampaging through them, consumed with the severe ache in their loins. Necking, groping, fumbling. So turned on with lust for each other they were lost to time and space.

Adam recalled the frenzy, the unbearable pain of being unable to finish what they'd started when they heard her roommate's key turn in the lock. He'd been so damned excited. Getting so close yet being held at bay. His penis had felt as if it would explode.

He'd thought they'd lost that level of intensity, that kind of novel excitement. His labored breathing and heightened sensation brought it all back, and the resulting flood of memories shoved his arousal even higher.

Thrusting his tongue past her lips, he explored the tasty landscape of her warm, hungry mouth. Pushing his hardness toward her, he clasped a hand at the crotch of her panties.

Morgan braced herself against the thick stone balustrade of the balcony and opened her legs wider. She slid her fingers over his, pressing him against her.

She was so hot and wet. Dripping juicily for him.

With his fingers and palm he massaged her hot mound, circling, teasing, trying a new move. Adam watched her face to see if she liked it. She quivered, eyes closed, and smiled.

Using his free hand, he trailed fingertips over her breasts swollen with desire. Gently he squeezed her tender flesh, heard her moan in delight.

He forgot his own need and got wrapped up in hers instead. He wanted to give her the biggest orgasm he'd ever given her. Wanted to watch her scream his name over and over again.

Her face softened and her breath quickened. He watched her float on the pleasure he was giving her with his hands, saw her seek the joy of the rapture he offered.

All he cared about was making her happy. If he never had another orgasm again, he could live with that as long as she was satisfied.

Morgan jerked against his hand and Adam recognized the first sign of her impending orgasm. Her internal muscles clenched tightly around his fingers, and he felt it radiating from her feminine center, spreading out through the innermost part of her.

Guttural sounds slipped from her lips, sexy, animalistic moans as wave upon wave of release rolled and pitched inside her.

And then she crumpled heavily into his embrace.

He held her, cooing soft words of love into her ear as he scooped her in his arms and carried her to bed.

They lay lazily together on top of the covers, holding hands as he spooned his body around hers. It had been a long time since they'd cuddled like this, and he hadn't realized how much he missed the closeness.

This kind of contact, gentle and loving, warmed him in a way that mere sex could not. A feeling grew in him. Of wonder and goodness and rightness with the world. It was not the same feeling he got when he snagged a big client or bought something he'd been longing to afford. This feeling was deeper, rich, more important than the short rush of endorphins he got from winning a competition or closing a big business deal.

Adam experienced the simple, basic goodness of being alive and in the arms of the woman he loved.

He felt imbued with a special presence, an inner glow radiating outward. It was the kind of feeling he struggled hard to capture with his achievement, but somehow he always fell short no matter how well he succeeded.

As he lay there with his wife, he felt transcendent and at the very same time grounded and very human.

Morgan stroked the back of his hand with her thumb, tickling him softly, and he pressed his lips against her bare shoulder. Grateful, he was so grateful that she was his wife.

Morgan rolled over to face him. Their eyes met and Adam's heart melted. She had stuck with him through thick and thin. She deserved so much more than what he'd been giving her.

She began to undress him, teasing him by brushing her bare breasts against his arm. She was taking over now, and he relinquished control, recognizing her need for more give and take in their relationship.

He reveled in the flame of her boldness. She eased his pants off his hips and then giggled over the extent of his arousal.

"Egmath, my love," she said. "I had no idea you were so enormous."

"Are you frightened, Batu?"

She licked her lips and winked. "Not at all."

"Saucy wench."

She sat beside him on the bed, her legs crossed tailor-style and lowered her head to gently tease the head of his penis with her tongue. She licked the rim of him, making him gasp and start. Her warm lips engulfed him and he felt himself swell larger still.

"Morgan," he groaned and threaded his fingers through her hair.

She paused just long enough to pull back and whisper, "I am Batu."

"Batu," Adam murmured, forcing his mind back on the role-playing game for her enjoyment. "Yes, my beloved, it is you."

She went back to her sweet licking, her passion shooting him to the stars. Firmly she suckled, taking him deeper and deeper into her mouth.

His breath caught in his throat and he feared his heart would stop. It felt that spectacular. What had he ever done to deserve a woman like her?

Her tongue performed magic on his excited flesh, and he was reborn. She had been right all along. She was so often right. Why didn't he listen to her more closely?

This was exactly what their marriage had been missing. Time away from the world and from the demands of their everyday routine. Time to rediscover each other. To remember what they'd been to each other in the first place. To refill their emotional well.

He sank into the covers, his body heavy as lead, heart pounding, his excitement expanding, growing more and more intense with each passing moment. He ached to touch her, caress her and kiss her. He reached out, but she blocked his hand.

"No," she said. "Enjoy and don't interrupt."

Not knowing what else to do, he relinquished all control.

Adam suddenly felt very awkward. As if he was with a new woman, a stranger. And in a way, he was. Morgan was different. She'd changed, and he was desperately afraid she wouldn't want him anymore.

That was a disturbing thought, but before he had time to examine it in his mind, the rush of sensation was so strong it consumed all his brain cells.

"Woman," he gasped, "what are you doing to me?"

She'd shifted from her lips to her hands and was swiftly but gently rubbing the head of his penis between her palms. The feeling was so incredible he almost lost consciousness.

"Making fire," she whispered. "Do you like it?"

"Sweetheart, I'm going up like a house ablaze." He was barely able to gasp out the words, barely made sense. "Where…in…the…hell…learn…trick?"

"A woman has to have a few secrets to keep her man guessing."

Secrets, hell. He'd known the woman for almost a dozen years and she was still a mystery to him.

His eyes rolled back in his head and he could speak no more. His body stiffened to marble. Just when he was about to explode, Morgan pulled her hands from him, leaving his body wet and burning for more of her.

She straddled him and he gasped aloud. Pushing up onto her knees, Morgan took him in her hand and guided his throbbing head into her slippery crease.

Adam slid a hand around her waist, anchoring her in place as she eased herself down over him, not stopping her descent until he was fully sheathed inside her hot, moist body.

Then, without warning, she pulled her body upward ever so slowly, halting only when it seemed that if she moved up one more millimeter he would slip away from her velvet grip.

Down, up, down, up. She increased the tempo until he could not stand one minute more.

"Stop," he croaked. "Stop now."

But it was too late. Adam grabbed her ass as he

exploded into her, hanging on for dear life. Torrents of his hot male essence streamed into her.

I hope I make you pregnant. I want to make you pregnant with my baby. Our baby.

Spent, he collapsed against the pillow, gasping for breath, but Morgan kept riding him hard until at last she, too, stiffened. Leaning back, holding her wrist to her mouth to muffle her cries of release, she tightened her muscles over him, trapping him inside her, not releasing him until the clutching spasm of her climax had subsided.

Then she leaned forward and fell against his shoulder. He clung to her, held her close.

And as he did, he realized it couldn't last. That this wonderful new intimacy was bound to shatter.

Because it was all based on a lie.

12

WHILE HIS WIFE SLEPT, Adam lay propped up on his elbow, looking down at her.

Her lashes were pale but long, brushing bristly crescents against her high cheekbones. Her mouth was slightly parted and her hair curled around her chin.

God, she was so beautiful.

He hadn't done a single thing to deserve her and yet he was directionless without her. She was the rudder to his ship, the wind in his sails. And he could not stay here and spoon with her in the bed no matter how badly he wanted to do so. He was obliged to tiptoe downstairs and find a place where he could phone Davidson in private.

He was giving half his attention to Criterion and half to Morgan, trying to please them both, but he had this horrible feeling of certainty that in the end he was going to please neither.

He felt like a hamster on a wheel, running, running, running, always running but never getting anywhere. He was always on, always producing. He was a master at altering himself to meet the image valued by a particular audience. He strived to be the perfect husband to Morgan, the perfect employee to Davidson.

But who was he really?

The hell of it was Adam had no answer.

He was coming unraveled and had no clue how to sew himself back up again.

Slowly Adam eased out of bed. When he was certain that he hadn't awakened Morgan, he slipped into his clothes. His fingers tightened around his cell phone, which he stuck into his front pocket, and then he grabbed the laptop. He opened the door and slipped out into the darkness of the hallway.

To quiet the doubt in his head, he started going through a list of contacts he had in Europe, people who could put him in touch with bankers or billionaires.

Yes, that was the answer. Focus on the task at hand. Do what was in front of you. Deal with one problem at a time.

Davidson was expecting his call.

Downstairs Adam found a secluded place in the lobby from which to make his call. It was almost midnight here. Only five in the afternoon in Manhattan. Taking a deep breath, Adam dialed Davidson's number.

"Paul," he said when his boss answered. "It's Adam Shaw."

Tell him, tell him, tell him.

"Talk to me. I need more details. Lots of details. The work you e-mailed me is not up to your usual high standards. What's going on?"

Adam cringed. He might as well just come out with

it. Get it over with. He knew the promotion was dead in the water. Deep down he'd known it from the minute he'd stepped on the plane for France.

"Paul, I've got to be honest with you. There's something you should know."

But Davidson went right on speaking as if he hadn't been listening to what Adam had said. "Jacobbi just called and he wants to meet with you tonight at the Grand Duchess. Eight o'clock. Can you make it?" Davidson asked.

"No."

"All right, then you call Jacobbi and tell him the meeting is no go. You smooth things over. Get this fixed."

"I can't do that either because I'm celebrating my tenth wedding anniversary in France with my wife."

"Excuse me?" He could almost hear Davidson's jaw drop.

Adam closed his eyes, steeling himself against the doubt and regret assailing him. He was doing what he had to do for his marriage. Morgan was more important than any job, any career, any duty would ever be.

"You took your vacation after I expressly told you not to?"

"Yes, sir, I did and I'm extremely sorry. I realize this means I won't be getting the promotion…."

"Let me stop you right there. You're a very valuable employee. I don't want to lose you. You're the hardest worker I have, so I'm cutting you some slack here, but you're right. The promotion is no longer on the table, but that's not the real issue here. If you're going to be on my team, you have to be on my team fully, completely. Here's the deal, Shaw. You either get on the next flight home out of Paris or you're fired."

MORGAN LAY NESTLED IN the down comforter, hands cradled under her head, staring up the ceiling, smiling and smiling and smiling. She'd known the minute Adam had slipped out of bed, but she didn't mind. Especially since that wonderfully romantic role-playing game of Egmath and Batu.

The game had been something of a pilgrimage for her. Adam had taken her three thousand years into the past and used her obsession with the star-crossed lovers to heighten their own lovemaking. He'd understood what she'd needed and he'd given it to her.

Magic.

The door creaked open and she turned her head to watch him walk in. Her heart did that crazy skittering thing it always did when she caught sight of him. Even after ten years he was still her one and only.

"Hey, handsome," she purred and patted the mattress beside her. "Come to bed and we'll make fire again."

"You're awake."

"Uh-huh."

"Good, that's good." He nodded his head and turned on the lamp beside the bed, but the look on his face was anything but good. He laid down his laptop on the table and ran his palms nervously over his pants.

She scooted up in bed and propped herself against the headboard. "What's wrong?"

"Morgan...I...there's something I have to tell you." Adam stuffed his hands in his pockets and shifted his weight. He was definitely nervous and not looking her in the eyes.

Her heart took a nosedive into her stomach. "Adam?"

Guilt weighted him. She could see it in the way his shoulders slumped, how he dropped heavily down on the opposite side of the bed from her.

"What did you do?"

Finally he met her eyes. "I lied to you."

"About what?" She splayed a hand over her throat, felt her pulse jump erratically.

"I didn't stand up to Davidson. I didn't tell him I was coming to France. I tried to bluff my way through it. I thought I'd come here for the weekend to please you and then convince you to come back home."

"And the only reason you even came after me in the first place was because you thought I was planning on having an affair with Henri Renouf."

Adam's face flushed brightly and he nodded. "I'm a total ass, Morgan. Everything that you said about me is true. My identity is wrapped up in my work. I get lost in it. So lost that I lied to you and I lied to Davidson. I pretended to him that I was working on Jacobbi's prospectus and I pretended to you that I was working on our marriage. The thing of it is, I wasn't working on either one and I just kept digging myself into a deeper hole."

She studied him a moment and then made a sad, mournful noise. "I should have known it was all too good to be true."

"Morgan, I'm sorry."

He reached for her, but she shied away from him, her heart was shredding in a thousand tiny pieces. "Please don't touch me right now. I'm feeling a little betrayed."

"I might have been less than honest with you but it doesn't change what happened here. We made a breakthrough in our marriage, I know we did."

"The breakthrough doesn't count, Adam. Not when it was based on a lie." She folded her arms over her chest and bit down on her bottom lip to keep it from quivering. Aw, hell.

"We had phenomenal sex," he pointed out. She could see him grasping at straws, trying to convince her. "That has to count for something."

"Yes, but phenomenal sex alone can't fix us, Adam. Making a relationship work—and I mean really work—entails completely risking your heart. No hesitation, no holding back, no lying to either me or yourself."

"I don't know what that means. Risking your heart? Tell me what that means. I love you. I've always loved you. If that's not risking your heart, then what is?"

"It means that you're an achievement machine, Adam. But your activities don't come from the heart. The more you chase the rat race, the more inauthentic you become. To the point where you're lying to me and lying to your boss just to keep running on that treadmill. Risk finding out what's inside your heart. Risk finding out who you really are and what you really want. Don't let your parents, your boss or even me tell you what you need."

Adam gulped audibly, and she found herself stupidly wanting to feel sorry for him. "I can't do that."

"Why not?"

"Because it scares the living hell out of me."

"Why does it scare you?"

"I don't know."

She leaned forward in the middle of the bed, forcing Adam to lean back against the headboard, cornering him with her intimacy. She stared into his eyes. Assessing. Sizing him up. Looking beyond the surface, peering deep inside. And she saw his terror.

He was afraid that she would see nothing of substance there. That there was no heart to risk. That drive and ambition and goals were all that comprised Adam Shaw.

She wanted to tell him it wasn't so, that he was so much more than he knew. But how did you convince someone of that? The silence stretching between them was like the pause at the end of a job interview—where decisions get made.

"You're afraid that if you let me see your weaknesses then I won't love you anymore." After ten years, she knew him so well. He couldn't hide himself from her.

He opened his mouth to deny it, but nothing came out.

"Here's the deal, Adam. Until you reawaken your heart, until you let me see the real you—fears, flaws and all—we can't fully, completely love each other in the way we both deserve to be loved."

He rummaged for the right response, she could see it on his face. "You think I should be able to magically pull feelings out of a hat, hold them up to the light, examine them, dissect them, make sense of them, but I don't know how to do that."

"Yes you do," she said. "You just won't be able to admit it until you learn to open your heart."

"My heart's open."

"Not fully. Not completely. But I love you anyway." Morgan kissed him lightly on the lips and was surprised when he flinched.

"That's not all. There's more."

"Oh?" She rocked back against the pillows, away from him.

"I have to go back home," he said. "First thing in the morning. If I don't, I'm fired."

"Davidson gave you an ultimatum?"

"Yeah. I'm calling the airline. Do you want me to book a seat for you, too?"

Morgan shifted her gaze to the box that was sitting on the dresser. She couldn't go. Not yet. Not now. This was as important to her as his job was to him. "What about the box? What about Egmath and Batu?"

"Egmath and Batu don't put food on the table, Morgan. I've already lost the VP position. If I don't go home, I'll lose my job, too."

"Maybe that's not such a bad thing."

He stared at her. "Are you nuts? You think losing my job isn't a bad thing?"

"It would be a good thing if you'd learn to let go and relax."

"You're being childish and demanding, expecting me to throw my job away on a whim."

"Do you consider our marriage a whim?"

"What are you saying?"

"I'm saying that maybe losing that job could be the best thing that ever happened to us."

"Losing the only career I've ever had is a very bad thing, dammit," he argued. He looked as if he'd stepped in quicksand and there was no way out.

"Not if it opens your heart to what it really is that you want to do with your life. Not if it helps you to find you."

He tossed his hands in the air. "I have no idea what you're talking about. My life is falling apart and you're babbling about risking my heart."

She felt as if he'd never really loved her. "I thought you could change, but I was wrong. You haven't been listening to a single word I've been saying. You're just as clueless as the day I left Connecticut."

"So what's the bottom line here?" he asked.

"That's all you're about. The bottom line. The profit margin. The brass ring. Oh, excuse me, in your case, the platinum ring."

Confusion was written across his face. "I don't get it. What else is there?"

She sank her face into her hands and gave a small

moan of despair. "I've been so stupid. I believed that because you came after me you were willing to take our relationship to a whole new level. But it was never about that, was it? This has been about winning. Winning me back, winning me away from a fictional lover. It's always about winning with you, isn't it?"

All he had to do to fix it was promise not to go back to New York. But by not going home he would lose everything he'd ever worked for. Ten years at Criterion down the tubes and she knew he would not do it.

"That's it." Morgan dusted her palms together. "I'm done fighting for your attention. Criterion wins. Take the convertible, go back to Paris tonight. Catch the first plane in the morning. I'll get the supersonic train to Nice tomorrow, rent a car from there and drive to Henri's villa. He'll be happy that I'm coming sooner than planned. At least he's interested in my box."

"What are you saying, Morgan?"

"I'm saying there's no magic between us. There never has been anything special. I've just been kidding myself all along. Trying to make something more out of our relationship than there is."

"That's not true," he argued. "We do have magic. We are special."

"Then prove it. Stay here with me."

"But I can't."

"That's exactly what I knew you would say." She looked at him and in that moment feared that their marriage was broken, shattered beyond repair.

13

SIX O'CLOCK ON TUESDAY morning Paris time, Adam stood in line, waiting to board his flight home. His heart was a fractured jigsaw puzzle. He'd ripped apart the fabric of his marriage and he had no idea at this point if it was fixable.

Reawaken your heart, Morgan had pleaded with him, but how did a man go about doing that?

Tentatively Adam splayed his palm over the left side of his chest, right over his heart, and took a few long, slow deep breaths.

Okay, dammit, reawaken. Show me what it is I'm missing. Why can't I get this?

He sat in the airport terminal and let his mind drift into his heart, let it engulf him, pounding, pumping, throbbing. He was inside his own heart and it was amazing. Tough and resilient and so full of love it scared him.

And vulnerable. His heart was so damned vulnerable.

As if burned, he dropped his hand, unnerved by what he'd discovered beating in his own chest. He did not understand what was happening to him, but he felt the changes occurring deep within his soul.

He'd been so competitive in his work that somewhere along the way, amidst winning and trying to get ahead, he'd gone flat emotionally.

From the time he was a small boy he'd been afraid of showing too much emotion. Maybe it came from having a strong corporate executive for a dad who told him boys had to be tough. He shouldn't cry, shouldn't let the world think he was weak. Maybe it had something to do with his fear that if he ever let himself feel too much, then he wouldn't be able to pursue his goal with the necessary determination.

The gate agent announced they were boarding his flight. Adam picked up his suitcase and got in line, his mind still turning his problem over.

Whatever the cause, he recognized the pattern now, saw he often put his wife in a no-win situation. He would either get impatient with Morgan for not understanding his need to throw himself wholeheartedly into his career or he would act so remote it was as if she wasn't really there at all.

For years Adam had worried obsessively about what "they" thought of him without ever defining who "they" were. And whose approval mattered more? Morgan's or this anonymous "they"?

She was right. He'd been hiding his real self. Afraid to let down his guard and show her who he really was. He was terrified she would see he was nothing more than fast talk and bravado.

That deep inside he was valueless. Empty.

The thing of it was, she had seen through all this and she loved him anyway.

He was so lucky to have her and he'd never fully appreciated it.

Go after her.

Duty versus love. He faced the same dilemma as Egmath. The ancient warrior had chosen duty.

And so had he.

But it was the wrong choice.

Adam was mentally debating his choices and stepping up next to have his boarding ticket taken by the gate agent when his cell phone rang.

Morgan! His heart leaped with hope.

He stepped away from the gate agent and moved to the back of the line again and he juggled his suitcase while he whipped the cell phone from his jacket pocket. He flipped it open and spoke without looking at the caller ID. "Morgan, sweetheart, you've got to forgive me."

"Adam?"

Immediately he recognized his sister-in-law's voice. "Cass?"

"I was calling Morgan's phone. Weird. Did I hit the wrong speed-dial button by mistake?"

He heard the sound of another phone ringing. In his other pocket. Hell, in his haste to get to Paris he must have mistakenly grabbed Morgan's phone again.

"Hold on a minute, Cass," he said. "I've got another call."

"This is extremely urgent, Adam."

"Okay, okay, one sec." He put her on hold, fished out the other cell and this time checked the caller ID. It was his boss.

He answered the phone. "What is it, Davidson?"

"Have you got on that plane yet?"

"I'm boarding now."

"Call me when you're in the air."

"You want me to charge the airplane phone to my expense account?"

"I want you on that damned plane, Shaw. If you weren't such a good worker, I wouldn't be putting up with this crap. Call me when you're in the air." Davidson hung up.

Adam gritted his teeth, went back to Cass waiting on Morgan's phone. "I'm here. Talk to me."

The guy behind him jostled Adam's elbow, urging him to move up in line. He motioned for him to go ahead.

"Adam, where's Morgan? Is she with you? I hope she's with you, but the way you answered the phone leads me to believe she's not with you."

"She's not with me," he said grimly.

Cass audibly sucked in her breath. Overhead the intercom announced final boarding for his flight to New York. Anxiously he shifted his weight as he watched the last passenger walk into the Jetway.

"What is it?" he asked. "What's wrong?"

"You know that antique collector Morgan is going to see?"

"Henri Renouf?"

"Yes."

"She's on her way to see him right now," he said.

"What? She's going alone?"

"We had a fight. I'm flying back home and she's headed to the south of France."

"She can't!" Cass exclaimed. "You've got to go after her, Adam. You've got to stop her from meeting Renouf."

"What is it?" His gut twisted.

Cass was breathless with concern. "Sam's just found out that not only did Henri Renouf originally commission the theft of the White Star but he's suspected of having the thief who stole it murdered. Renouf is a cold-blooded killer, Adam. And as we speak, my sister's life is in mortal danger."

MORGAN FELT AS IF THE hand of destiny had been pushing her here.

To this place. To this point in time. To uncover the mystery of the box, to find out what Egmath and Batu had to tell her.

The urge was so strong, so important, but the answers seemed to hover just beyond her understanding.

She propelled her tiny rental car south, oblivious to the beauty stretching out on either side of her. To her right lay the Mediterranean Sea, to her left, lush hillsides. Just ahead of her, nestled in a picturesque valley, was the fishing village where Henri Renouf kept a villa.

On the seat beside her rested the box that had started all the trouble. Until she'd discovered the box, dug into the legend of Egmath and Batu and become obsessed with what was inside, she'd been happy enough. Sure, there had been no magic in her life, but neither had there been this pit-of-her-stomach aching sorrow.

She had longed for a relationship like Egmath and Batu's, and that's exactly what she'd gotten.

A man who chose duty over love.

She sucked in her breath and hardened her chin. The pain stretched from the center of her abdomen all the way to her throat. She felt panicky, as if she'd strayed too close to the edge of a thin precipice and there was a storm brewing. Any moment the wind could kick up and she could tumble over and that would be the end of her.

What happened to us, Adam? How did it come to this?

Unexpected sensations assaulted her.

The feel of Adam's fingers whenever he would lift her hair from the nape of her neck and blow hot circles against her skin. Then kiss her there as if whispering an ancient story to her soul. The way he looked in the morning before he'd pulled on his persona, hair sticking up in tufts, eyes thick with sleep. How he always kept the car gassed up for her use and how he kept the snow shoveled off the walk in the winter. The wine-colored birthmark on the inside of his left wrist. And the endearing way he let her put her cold feet on his lower back to warm them up when she came to bed. How he liked elephant ears so much he'd planted too many in the front flower bed at home and they'd overtaken the tiger lilies.

All the little things she'd taken for granted, never noticed really, while she'd waited for him to do something magical, something grand, something startling to sweep her off her feet.

Was this what she'd wanted? This tortured torment? How sad that she could only feel the magnitude of his love for her as she was losing it.

She was almost there. She was within minutes of finding out the contents of the box. But instead of the excitement and joy she had expected to feel, Morgan felt emotionally flat. Empty, drained, devoid.

In the back of her mind she had convinced herself that if there was something in the box that proved Egmath and Batu's undying love for each other, there was hope for her and Adam. That together they could find that elusive magic.

But now she knew that wasn't true. No matter what was in the box, no matter how Egmath and Batu's love affair ended, it had nothing to do with her marriage. She'd been kidding herself. Spinning fantasies. Longing for something she had no business longing for.

She shouldn't have forced Adam to choose between going home to his job or coming with her.

An emotional desert lay in front of her, as real as the physical desert where Egmath and Batu had once lived. Because of her stubborn need to feel a grand passion, she'd placed everything in jeopardy. Her husband, his love, their marriage. She had been so nearsighted, yearning for some special kind of magic, when in reality she'd been in possession of it all along.

In that moment she almost turned around and went back to Paris to catch the next flight home.

But then she saw it.

Henri Renouf's villa perched high on a hill above the sleepy little fishing village.

All Egmath and Batu's secrets would soon be revealed. Perhaps in that box she would find the answers she so desperately sought. She hoped it was so. She hoped all of this had not been for naught.

She'd come this far, her marriage was already hanging on by a thread and Adam was on his way home. She might as well see this journey to the end.

HENRI RENOUF IS A cold-blooded killer.

Cass's words echoed loudly in his head as Adam boarded the high-speed train that ran from Paris to Nice. With any luck, he would arrive at the fishing village not long after Morgan did.

"Please, God, let me be in time," he prayed.

Before she hung up, Cass had assured Adam that Sam would try to notify MI6, who'd had Renouf under investigation, and tell them what was going on. But would it all happen in time?

Adam felt no comfort.

He'd left Morgan to travel to Renouf's alone. He'd chosen his work over her. He had called her childish and demanding when all she had wanted was his attention. The pain of his shameful behavior cut like a finely honed sword, stabbing up through his gut and into his heart.

All she had wanted was two weeks of magic, and he'd been unable to grant her even that simple request. And now he stood to lose her forever.

And all for what?

A job. His male ego. His idiotic need to preserve his good image at all costs.

It all seemed so stupidly unimportant in the face of real danger.

Why had he not realized before, not just how much he loved Morgan but how much he needed her? She was his tower of strength. She was his heart, his soul, his conscience, his destiny. If anything happened to her, he would surely be ruined, his life empty and useless without her guiding hand.

He would not, could not, let anything happen to her. He would die first.

Morgan, Morgan, Morgan. Her name beat a hole in his brain. He had to get to his wife.

And on the two-hour trip to Nice on the train, not once, not for a single minute, did Adam ever think about Criterion or Jacobbi or his job.

THE LATE-MORNING SKY was blue as a jay's wing as Morgan climbed the stone pathway leading to Henri Renouf's villa, Egmath and Batu's box tucked safely in her tote bag. The sea stretched out like a silk carpet across the shadowy walkway, and the air smelled rich and fresh. It was such a beautiful view, and she couldn't help feeling sorry that Adam was not here to enjoy it with her.

She stared up at the front of the elaborate stone mansion surround by a slope of trees still verdant in early September. As the hairs on her forearms prickled, she had the sensation that she was being watched and found herself scanning the terrain around her.

But there was nothing.

She found herself pausing, looking up at the majestic house on the cliff, of two minds, caught between her curiosity and an almost overwhelming desire to turn and run.

She might even have left if someone hadn't called out to her.

"*Bonjour.* Madame Shaw?"

Shading her eyes with her hands against the glare of the morning sun, she gazed at the man who had appeared at the top of the stairs. "*Bonjour,* Monsieur Renouf."

The man, dressed in an expensive silk suit, walked long-limbed toward her. "*Mais non,* I am Tomas Solange," he said in English. "Monsieur Renouf's antiquities expert in North African cultures."

"Oh," she said. "I thought Monsieur Renouf was the expert."

"Monsieur Renouf's interests are too numerous for him to be a scholar in every field of study." He held out his hand to her. "Please, this way. Watch your step. *Monsieur* is waiting in the solarium for you."

Tomas Solange guided her inside the elegant stone house. It was hundreds of years old, but no money had been spared keeping it restored in pristine condition. Morgan gazed with interest as they wandered through the hall toward the solarium. There they found Henri Renouf, dressed in a pretentious blue serge suit, sitting at a white wicker table with a tea service beside him. She had the distinct feeling the entire scene had been carefully set up for her benefit.

Tomas introduced them and then stepped back among the numerous potted plants that were drinking in the sunlight from the wide-paned windows.

"My dear Mrs. Shaw, it is a great pleasure to meet you," Renouf said and extended his hand. When she reached out to shake it, he held on to her hand, lifted it to his mouth and lightly kissed her knuckles. She found the continental custom creepy and couldn't wait to get her hand back.

"It is my good fortune to make your acquaintance."

"The fortune is all mine." Renouf was a short, balding man with intelligent but cold eyes. He was older than she'd thought he would be, even though he clearly dyed his hair to appear younger. "Would you like a cup of tea?"

"Very much, thank you."

He poured them both a cup of tea from the tea service, all without taking his eyes off her. It was as if he expected her to run away at any moment.

"Forgive my anxiousness to dispense with the pleasantries," he said as he pushed the cream and sugar bowls toward her and eyed her tote bag speculatively. "But did you bring the box with you?"

"Do you have the White Star?" she volleyed back.

His tight-lipped smile was appreciative. "I do."

He snapped his fingers over his shoulder at Tomas, and the man placed the something in his hand.

That's when Morgan saw the White Star for the first time. She drew in a breath as he laid the amulet on the table between them.

It was very plain but unbelievably compelling. She could not take her eyes off it. Made of ivory in the shape of a five-pointed star, with a hollowed-out center so it could be worn on a strap or chain around the neck.

To think, this was the amulet Batu had commissioned for her beloved Egmath to forever remember the awesome power of their cosmic love. She scarcely dared breathe and her fingers itched to touch it. She reached out, but Renouf quickly closed his fist around it.

She looked up to find a wicked gleam in his beady dark eyes. "The box," he said.

Nodding, Morgan wet her lips. The time had come. At last, at long last, the contents of the box would be revealed. She took the box from her tote bag and laid it on the table beside the amulet.

"Do you know how to open it?" Renouf asked.

"Yes," she said and thought of what Cate Wells's expert archaeologist had said.

"Then you may have the honor." Renouf indicated the box with a flourish.

Tentatively she picked up both the box and the White Star. The amulet represented Egmath. The box, Batu.

She looked at Renouf, surprised to find herself in this luxury villa in the south of France with this man.

They were two people who would likely have never met. They only had one thing in common: their shared lust for the legend of the star-crossed lovers and all that it represented.

Oddly, she now suddenly felt as if her entire life had been building to this climatic moment.

Henri nodded. "Go on."

With trembling fingers Morgan slipped the White Star into the carved grooves, where it fit perfectly. The hollow center actually anchored the amulet. Using her fingertips, she pressed tightly and rotated the amulet one full turn as the box clicked and snapped and then sprang open in her hands.

HURRY, HURRY. FASTER. FASTER.

Adam's fear was a living thing in his chest, scrambling, clawing, demanding. If Renouf had killed over the legend and the amulet, Adam had no doubt he would do it again.

"Morgan's okay, she's alive," he kept muttering to himself over and over as he barreled the car he'd rented in Nice down the narrow winding road toward the fishing village where Henri Renouf lived. He had to say it to make himself believe it. Had to believe it or go mad.

His heart knocked so hard and fast that his ears were filled with the constant strumming. He kept thinking of what Cass had told him, what he'd let Morgan walk into.

"Dear God," he prayed. "Please let her be okay. If

you let her be okay, I swear that I'll spend the rest of my life being the kind of man she needs me to be."

He saw the villa on the cliff overlooking the sea, and sweat broke out on his forehead. He was in time. He had to be in time.

"Hang in there, sweetheart," he said aloud and pushed the foot pedal all the way down. "I'm coming, I'm coming."

RENOUF'S BREATH WAS hot against her neck. Morgan had been so absorbed in opening the box that she hadn't realized Renouf had come to stand behind her chair and that he was peering over her shoulder, crowding her personal space.

Inside the box lay a small piece of yellowed parchment folded into a square and stamped with sealing wax. Alongside of it rested a scroll of unsealed parchment.

Before she could even react to her find, Renouf snatched up the scroll, unrolled it and frowned at the symbols scrawled there. "Tomas," he commanded, thrusting the parchment at his employee. "Read what this says."

Tomas did his best to cobble together a translation of the writing, reading the legend of Egmath and Batu from the scroll. The letter told of the lovers' secret rendezvous and how Batu had fashioned the star-shaped amulet of the purest ivory, for Egmath, to remember her by. White symbolized the goodness of their souls, and the shape of the star symbolized hope that eternal love would eventually win out. It went on to describe the night they had made love for the first and only time and how the amulet had blazed brightly and held the power of true love for whoever possessed it and was pure of heart.

"Ah," Renouf said and rubbed his palms together. "I possess it now. The power of true love belongs to me."

Morgan stared at him, uneasiness rippling her skin. The man's eyes gleamed with a disturbed light.

Tomas kept piecing together the wording. Egmath married Princess Anan, the older sister, the following morning, and not long after the marriage was made, Egmath and his army were called upon to fight in a faraway land. An epic battle ensued and Egmath was killed. But he had created a special box in case this happened that could only be opened with the amulet, to ensure that his letter traveled safely back to Batu and that its sanctity went unbroken. He had instructed his closest friend and one of his commanders, Arik, to deliver it to Batu upon his death.

It was Arik who had penned the scroll. At the end of the letter was a postscript saying that the sealed parchment was for Batu's eyes only and he, Arik, had been appointed by Egmath as the keeper of their secret, and it was up to his descendents to make sure the sacred trust was never violated.

"The name Arik," Tomas said as an aside, "translates into the modern-day equivalent of the name Richards."

That's my maiden name, Morgan thought.

Could she possibly be some distant descendent of

Arik, the first protector of the White Star? The thought was jarring. Was something mystical at work here? Was that why she'd been so captivated by the legend? Why she'd felt as if destiny's hand were guiding her here? Could the need to protect the sacred trust between Arik and Egmath be part of her genetic code? It was a fanciful notion but she felt it deep inside her gut. Whether an ancestral connection to Arik was true or not, she knew in her heart that it was her duty to prevent the private letter from Egmath to his beloved Batu from being disturbed.

Renouf leaned over her shoulder and reached for the sealed parchment square. "Give me."

This pig wanted to read it as if it was a shopping list or the phone bill. She was disgusted, and the need to protect the legend called to something deep inside her.

She slapped a hand around Renouf's wrist. "You have no right to open it," she exclaimed. "None at all."

"I have every right," he rebuked her. "I've earned it. I've been after that amulet for a long time. It has cost me much in many ways and led me to something even more dear—this box and that love letter—and I won't let some disappointed housewife take it from me now."

In that moment she realized the man was a psychopath who in his twisted mind wanted the amulet and the box simply because he wanted them. She could see from the greedy expression in his simian eyes that he had an insatiable need to own, possess and dominate.

She had betrayed the memory of Egmath and Batu by coming here, by letting this horrible man get anywhere near the sacred parchment Egmath had written for Batu's eyes only.

This is it, she thought. *This is officially the bleakest moment of my life.*

"I will not let you open this letter," she declared.

"I'm afraid, my dear Mrs. Shaw, that you have no choice." He made a grab for the box and got hold of it, but she held on tight.

They pulled it between them in a crazy tug-of-war. Renouf was old, but he was strong and he would not let go. Morgan felt her fingers slipping. No, no. She wrenched hard, trying to throw Renouf off balance.

"Help me," Renouf cried out to Tomas.

But his employee was disappearing out the side door.

That's when Morgan heard it. Shouting in the hallway. Someone calling her name.

Adam!

Her heart leaped with joy.

"Adam!" she screamed. "Adam, I'm in here!"

He'd come to her. In her greatest hour of need, her husband had found her and come to save her.

Renouf let go of the box.

Ha! She cradled it to her chest, but her victory was short-lived.

Renouf stepped over to the tea service cart, opened the top drawer and pulled out a pistol. "Give me the box."

"No."

"Morgan!"

Morgan stared, horrified, when Renouf leveled the gun at Adam as he burst through the door.

Their eyes met in an instant, and every bit of love she'd ever felt for him was concentrated in one tight, precious ball and embedded deep within her chest.

"Morgan," he said.

"Adam."

A powerful energy arced between them. Love of the strongest kind. Pure, eternal, unconditional love.

"Ah, isn't this so precious," Renouf said. "True love and all that bunk wins out. Too bad you both have to be disposed of." Quickly he swung the weapon around to point it at Morgan's head. "But I think I'll take your wife out first, just so you can know the pain of watching her die."

Her blood turned to ice as the sound of Renouf cocking the pistol filled the air with a deadly ratcheting click.

"No!" Adam shouted and leaped between her and Renouf just as an echoing bang reverberated throughout the room.

She heard her beloved husband cry out, saw his big, strong, athletic body crumple to the ground. *Dear God, no, no!*

"Adam!" she shrieked and launched herself at Renouf.

He made a gasping noise as she knocked him to the ground. The pistol flew from his hand, spun across the floor.

"You bastard!" She pummeled him with her fists. "You shot him."

Renouf raised his arms defensively, howling like a wounded animal.

Distantly she heard more noises, voices, people talking somewhere in the house, but she wasn't listening. Everything within her hovered in the moment, in what was directly in front of her.

All those years of being a good girl, of doing what was expected of her, of living up to the perfect image, exploded in a backlash of anger and sorrow and revenge. She was a woman possessed. Renouf managed to get on all fours. She saw that he was crawling for the pistol. She clung to his back, determined not to let him get it.

He bucked.

She slid off his back.

He scurried to the gun, managed to wrap a hand around it, but she was on top of him again.

"Oh, no you don't," Morgan growled and bit down viciously on his wrist.

Renouf caterwauled and dropped the gun.

Morgan grabbed for it, but Renouf jammed an elbow in her ribs. She cried out in pain.

He snatched the gun up again and, with a shout of triumph, shoved the barrel in her face.

She might be a dead woman, but she did not care. The only thing she cared about in the entire world had been lost forever.

"Go ahead," she dared. "Shoot me. Without my husband, life isn't worth living."

"It's my pleasure to accommodate your request."

Grinning viciously, Renouf cocked the gun for the second time that day.

But again, they were interrupted.

Feeling surreally calm, Morgan flicked a gaze toward the intruders. It was two men and a woman dressed in fatigues. The woman was in the lead. All three held semiautomatic weapons. Their appearance registered as only a mild surprise to her shocked system.

"MI6. Henri Renouf, you are under arrest for the murder of Jean Luc Allard, the man you hired to steal the White Star from the Stanhope auction house in Manhattan." The woman, who possessed a smart British accent, barked. "Put down the gun. Now. Or I'll kill you myself."

14

IT TURNED OUT THAT while Adam had taken a bullet to the shoulder the wound had been minimized by immediate medical care and excellent medical care at that.

MI6 took their statements and carted Renouf off to prison. They kept the White Star amulet and the box as evidence in the investigation, but the woman MI6 agent allowed Morgan to keep the sealed parchment of Egmath's letter to Batu. When she and Adam got home, Morgan would put it in a safe-deposit box, pending the return of her antique box.

They went home to Connecticut the following day. And while Davidson indeed fired Adam for not getting on that plane, neither she nor Adam cared. They had each other and that was all that mattered.

But, to Adam's surprise, one of the contacts he'd made while in France came through as Jacobbi's major lender. Jacobbi Enterprises went public, and Jacobbi hired Adam as CFO of his company with only one stipulation: that Adam work no more than forty hours a week.

Two weeks later, after the hubbub had died down,

Adam walked into their house in Fairfield with two gift-wrapped packages in his hands.

Morgan stopped putting the groceries away and ran to wrap her arms around his neck. "What do you have there, big guy?"

"Presents."

"For me?" She giggled.

"Who else?"

"What's the occasion?"

"Well, we never did get to actually celebrate our wedding day. The moment was sort of overshadowed by me getting shot by Renouf. Here, open this one first."

She pulled the ribbon off the smaller package and opened it up to find a lavender cell phone inside. "A new cell phone, thanks."

"Because we kept getting our other phones mixed up."

"But, hey, that was a good thing. If you hadn't taken my phone and Cass hadn't called you..." Morgan shuddered. "I hate to think what would have happened."

"But if Cass had gotten hold of you, then you never would have gone to Renouf's in the first place."

"Point taken."

"Hang on a second. I'm going to call you."

"What for?"

"So you can hear the ringtone."

He pulled out his own cell phone and called her. The lavender phone played "Lara's Theme" from *Dr. Zhivago*. Morgan laughed.

"Now," he said, "when you get it in your head that

things are too ordinary between us, just call your own phone for a dose of tortured longing."

"I've learned my lesson. No more tortured longing for me."

She had learned a lot. Over the course of their French adventure Morgan had discovered that life was a series of challenges and rewards and that she hadn't made a mistake by choosing Adam as her mate. The problems they'd faced in their marriage weren't bad things but rather obstacles that facilitated emotional growth.

Without those difficulties and all that they'd shared together, she would not be the woman she was today. However many ups and downs, however many sweet, quiet moments versus vast emotional upheaval they shared, there was still that unknown realm to lure them in. If uncertainty was the essence of romance, there would always be enough variables to make love sizzle and renew their sense of wonder.

She thrilled to the fact that no matter how much she and Adam delved into each other there would always be some small part that would remain inscrutable. It was the spice of life.

This was indeed the great affair of which she'd always dreamed. She'd learned how to live as fully as possible and to groom her curiosity and make magic from the ordinary. Where there was nothing to gamble, the emotional territory was flat and fallow. How much better to travel valleys and hills, experience detours and potholes along the way. That was what made life worth living.

"Now," he said, "open the other one."

She unwrapped it to find the antique box. "You got it back? But I thought we wouldn't get it back for months and months, until Renouf's case came up for trial."

"It's not Egmath and Batu's box," he said. "It's our box."

She ran her fingers over the whiskered symbols and lettering. "But it looks exactly like it."

"I had it duplicated from those pictures the archaeologist took of it. I've been thinking, maybe we should donate the real box to the Louvre. It seems sort of fitting."

"Hmm," she said. "I like it. So what's in our box?"

He pulled a replica of the White Star from his pocket. "Why don't you open it and find out?"

Eagerly she opened the box he'd commissioned just for her and found a square piece of paper sealed with wax inside. She looked up and met her husband's eyes.

"It's my interpretation of the letter Egmath wrote to his true love," he said. "It's what I would have written if I was Egmath and you were Batu."

Stomach quivering, she broke the sealing wax, unfolded the letter and began to read.

My dearest beloved Morgan,
If you but knew how my heart is filled with love
for you. How the tender light in your eyes thrills
me in the night. How when others speak, it's your

voice I hear, whispering secret words for my ears only. Could you even begin to guess how you make up my happiness?

Your eternal love,

Adam

To think that her goal-oriented, unpoetic, thoroughly modern man had taken the time and trouble to commission this box and write her this letter.

What she'd mistaken as Adam's desire to numb his feelings with work was actually a demonstration of his commitment to her. He worked hard to be a success in her eyes and her dissatisfaction with the amount of time he spent with her versus is work was a blow to his self-esteem. She liked that he was successful and that he could take care of her and any children they might one day have. She admired his ability to multitask and still manage to do top flight work on anything he attempted. He had so many great qualities.

She found the magic had been there all along, right under her nose. She'd been looking for fireworks and that's not where it was at. It wasn't in the fancy anniversary celebrations or the things he bought her. It was in the sweet moments where magic really resided. A caress, a look, a whisper.

"I'll never be more than half a human being without you, Morgan," Adam said. "Can you forgive me for being such a thickheaded dolt?"

"Of course I forgive you, if you forgive me." Tears misted her eyes as she ran her hand over the box. "This is the most precious gift you've ever given me."

He held her close and kissed that spot on her jawline that made her toes curl. She smiled against the pressure of his lips. Just the smell of him caused her blood to rush, a hot flash flood of passion ripping through her veins.

Ah, yes, here was the passion, real and ripe and raging.

Morgan had no fear that they would ever slip back into their old patterns of taking the ordinary for granted and not living fully in the present, because the box Adam had commissioned for her would be on prominent display in their bedroom. A constant reminder of how much they loved each other and what they'd almost lost.

The experiences they'd been through had taught them the value of reveling in each other's company. In both good times and bad. Through all the little ups and downs. Through the magic moments and the quiet ones alike. Because there would be both, and she knew they could weather any storm and come out on the other side to the happiness waiting beyond. The lesson had been brutal, but they'd learned it well.

He unbuttoned her blouse. She pulled his polo shirt over his head. Simultaneously they kicked out of their shoes and shucked off their jeans.

They kissed hungrily, drinking with honeyed tongues. They played for a while, nipping and teasing and licking and tasting. She studied his face while he took off her bra. She never got tired of looking at that beautiful face.

She let out a throaty cry as he dropped his head to suckle her breast, and his control broke. He pulled her down on the kitchen table, sweeping the last of the groceries to the floor.

"I hope you didn't buy eggs," he said.

She just laughed.

They gazed longingly into each other's eyes, memorizing what they found there.

"I'll love you long past the time my heart stops beating," Adam said. "Through eternity."

"And beyond," she whispered.

Then, as their bodies found their perfect rhythm, they stopped talking and just lived the moment, fully embracing the magic.

And as they made love right there on the kitchen table, Morgan looked over and caught a glimpse of the White Star amulet Adam had made for her special box. It was probably just her imagination, but she could have sworn that just as they came together, the amulet glowed brightly.

Egmath and Batu, she decided.

They approved.

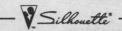

SPECIAL EDITION™

Welcome to Danbury Way—where nothing is as it seems...

Megan Schumacher has managed to maintain a low profile on Danbury Way by keeping the huge success of her graphics business a secret. But when a new client turns out to be a neighbor's sexy ex-husband, rumors of their developing romance quickly start to swirl.

THE RELUCTANT CINDERELLA

by CHRISTINE RIMMER

Available July 2006

Don't miss the first book from the Talk of the Neighborhood miniseries.

Visit Silhouette Books at www.eHarlequin.com   SSETRC

HOTEL MARCHAND

Four sisters.
A family legacy.
And someone is out to destroy it.

**A captivating new limited
continuity, launching June 2006**

The most beautiful hotel in New Orleans,
and someone is out to destroy it. But mystery,
danger and some surprising family revelations
and discoveries won't stop the Marchand sisters
from protecting their birthright…
and finding love along the way.

www.eHarlequin.com

HMC0606

SPECIAL PRICE!

This riveting new saga begins with

In the Dark

by national bestselling author

JUDITH ARNOLD

The party at Hotel Marchand is in full swing when the lights suddenly go out. What does head of security Mac Jensen do first? He's torn between two jobs—protecting the guests at the hotel and keeping the woman he loves safe.

A woman to protect. A hotel to secure. And no idea who's determined to harm them.

On Sale June 2006

**Hidden in the secrets of antiquity,
lies the unimagined truth...**

Introducing

**ROGUE
ANGEL**™

a brand-new line filled with mystery
and suspense, action and adventure,
and a fascinating look into history.

And it all begins with DESTINY.

In a sealed crypt in
France, where the
terrifying legend of
the beast of Gevaudan
begins to unravel,
Annja Creed discovers
a stunning artifact
that will seal her destiny.

*Available every other
month starting
July 2006, wherever
you buy books.*

**GOLD
EAGLE**®

GRA1

If you enjoyed what you just read,
then we've got an offer you can't resist!

Take 2 bestselling love stories FREE!

Plus get a FREE surprise gift!

Clip this page and mail it to Harlequin Reader Service®

IN U.S.A.	IN CANADA
3010 Walden Ave.	P.O. Box 609
P.O. Box 1867	Fort Erie, Ontario
Buffalo, N.Y. 14240-1867	L2A 5X3

YES! Please send me 2 free Harlequin® Blaze™ novels and my free surprise gift. After receiving them, if I don't wish to receive anymore, I can return the shipping statement marked cancel. If I don't cancel, I will receive 6 brand-new novels each month, before they're available in stores! In the U.S.A., bill me at the bargain price of $3.99 plus 25¢ shipping and handling per book and applicable sales tax, if any*. In Canada, bill me at the bargain price of $4.47 plus 25¢ shipping and handling per book and applicable taxes**. That's the complete price and a savings of at least 10% off the cover prices—what a great deal! I understand that accepting the 2 free books and gift places me under no obligation ever to buy any books. I can always return a shipment and cancel at any time. Even if I never buy another book from Harlequin, the 2 free books and gift are mine to keep forever.

151 HDN D7ZZ
351 HDN D72D

Name	(PLEASE PRINT)	
Address	Apt.#	
City	State/Prov.	Zip/Postal Code

Not valid to current Harlequin® Blaze™ subscribers.

Want to try two free books from another series?
Call 1-800-873-8635 or visit www.morefreebooks.com.

* Terms and prices subject to change without notice. Sales tax applicable in N.Y.
** Canadian residents will be charged applicable provincial taxes and GST.
All orders subject to approval. Offer limited to one per household.
® and ™ are registered trademarks owned and used by the trademark owner and/or its licensee.

BLZ05   ©2005 Harlequin Enterprises Limited.

Baseball. The crack of the bat,
the roar of the crowd…and the view
of mouthwatering men in tight uniforms!
A sport in which the men are men…
and the women are drooling.

Join three Blaze bestselling authors in
celebrating the men who indulge in this
all-American pastime—and the women
who help them indulge in other things….

Boys of Summer

A Hot (and Sweaty!) Summer Collection

One book, three great stories!

FEVER PITCH
by Julie Elizabeth Leto
THE SWEET SPOT by Kimberly Raye
SLIDING HOME by Leslie Kelly

On sale this July
Feel the heat. Get your copy today!

www.eHarlequin.com

HBBOSJUL